Goodbye, Excuses

Ian Wilfred

Goodbye, No More Excuses
Copyright © 2018 by Ian Wilfred

This is a work of fiction. Names, characters, places and incidents are used fictitiously and any resemblance to persons living or dead, business establishments, events, locations or areas, is entirely coincidental.

No part of this work may be used or reproduced in any manner without written permission of the author, except for brief quotations and segments used for promotion or in reviews.

ISBN: 978 1986661560

Cover Design: Avalon Graphics
Editing: Nancy Callegari
Proofreading: Maureen Vincent-Northam
Formatting: Rebecca Emin
All rights reserved.

For Ron

Acknowledgements

There are a few people I'd like to thank for getting *Goodbye, No More Excuses* out into the world.

The fabulous Rebecca Emin at Gingersnap Books for organising everything for me and who also produced both kindle and paperback books. Nancy Callegari for all the time and effort she spent editing the book, Maureen Vincent-Northam for proofreading, and the very talented Cathy Helms at Avalon Graphics for producing the terrific cover.

Finally for my late mum who is always with me in everything I do.

Chapter 1

Sandra felt like it had been the perfect summer's day, doing the things she loved most in life – pottering around in the garden all day, chatting, drinking tea and swapping plants with her neighbours. She considered herself so blessed to live in a lovely little cul-de-sac of bungalows among people of her own age who all shared a common love of gardening.

It was now nine o'clock in the evening, and Sandra had finally retired inside, poured herself a glass of wine and was starting to reminisce over the 20 years since the death of her husband. There was a time when she thought her life was over and she would be unable to be happy again, but now she felt so fortunate. She had lovely friends and most importantly, a very caring son and daughter-in-law.

Sandra was just deciding whether to switch on the television when the telephone rang.

"Hi, Mum. How are you?"

"Hello, Paul. Yes, I'm fine thanks. I've been in the garden as we've had such beautiful weather again."

"Mum, I'm going to pop around tomorrow. Will you be in all day?"

"Oh, that would be nice. Is Caroline coming with you? I'll cook us something."

"No, Caroline will be at work. Don't go to the

trouble of cooking. I'll see you about eleven if that's alright."

"That will be lovely, Paul. See you tomorrow. Bye for now."

As she put the phone down Sandra wondered whether something wasn't quite right. She was always one to worry about things and couldn't stop herself from thinking about it. Perhaps Paul and Caroline were planning a holiday like the one in Greece where they took her with them last year, or the year before that when they all went to France. Sandra had been away on holiday with Paul and Caroline for the last ten years. Few women would look forward to going on holiday with their mother-in-law every year and Sandra knew she was lucky to have such a lovely daughter-in-law. Caroline had become more of a best friend to her.

***

"Mum's expecting me at eleven tomorrow. Oh, Caroline, how can I tell her? It's going to break her heart. It doesn't need to be like this. We can sort it out. I really promise it will never happen again. Can't we just talk it over?"

"Paul, we've been going over and over this for a whole month. I'm sorry, but it's the end. I can't take any more of this. The problem with our marriage has been there for nearly twenty years and I've forgiven you more times than I care to remember. I need to move on and start again. The hurt you've caused me is something you'll never understand."

***

It was 7.30 and Sandra had been up for an hour. Although Paul had said that he didn't want anything to eat, Sandra loved being a perfect hostess and entertaining her friends and family. She would far prefer to cook for guests than be taken out for a meal and over the years had taught Caroline how to cook many dishes and make it all seem so effortless. There was already a sponge cake baking in the oven and now Sandra was making pastry for her famous Cornish pasties.

Caroline meant far more than a daughter-in-law to Sandra. They were very close friends and often spent the day doing things together, especially shopping, when Sandra caught the bus into Norwich and met Caroline from her early hotel shift. They would then browse around the shops, stop off for tea and cakes, and perhaps go to the theatre or the cinema. They enjoyed the same hobbies and really took pleasure in their days together.

Sponge out of the oven and cooling before the jam and cream goes on, pasties now cooking. A quick tidy up and a check on the garden. Sandra wondered how she had ever found the time to go to work. She had loved her job and worried about being lonely in her retirement, but despite missing her work colleagues life had never been better.

Chapter 2

ONE MONTH EARLIER

It had started as just a normal day off work for Caroline – coffee and toast and a flick through her iPad for ideas on interior design. Caroline loved her home and was passionate about keeping it modern and up to date with new pictures, cushions and ornaments. Her favourite designer was Kelly Hoppen, the queen of everything modern and homely and Caroline was slightly obsessed with her style and products as well as the way she worked and ran her business. She was just looking at rugs on a French website when the post arrived. It would have been perfect if she had received the catalogue she requested, but sadly there was only an official letter addressed to her and Paul from the bank. More junk mail, she thought.

The bank letter informed them that as they had defaulted on their loan payments, they needed to pay back the entire loan and asked them to come into the bank to discuss the matter. Caroline felt as if her head was about to explode. What loan? They didn't have a loan as their house was fully paid for and apart from credit cards which they paid off at the end of each month, they didn't owe any money to anyone.

"Not again, Paul. Please tell me it's not happening. I really can't take any more of this."

An hour or so later and after several coffees, Caroline decided there was no talking to Paul and listening to excuse after excuse. This needed to be resolved for the last time. There was no going back, starting again was not an option this time. All the time she had known Paul he had been a gambling addict. He would bet on anything, so why did she fool herself into thinking he would stop? One phone call to the bank and an appointment was made for that afternoon. Caroline needed to prepare for the worst.

Walking back into her beautiful home five hours later, Caroline knew exactly what she needed to do. There would be no shouting and certainly no tears. There had been far too much of that already over the previous 20 years. She just needed to dot the i's, and cross the t's for a new beginning for both of them. However, she needed to stay strong and in control for the first time ever in their relationship. She would not allow words like 'sorry' and 'it won't happen again' to enter into the equation.

"Hi, Caroline, I'm home. How was your day off? What have you been doing?"

"I'm in the dining room, Paul. Can you come in as we need to discuss a few things?"

"What's all the paperwork for? It's like sitting down in my accountant's office. What's going on here?"

"Well, Paul, it is a bit like being at the accountant's as we need to sort out a few money issues. I need you to sit down and not speak until I have finished all I have to say. I mean it, not a bloody word or else I will not be responsible for my actions. Do I make myself clear? Not one word until I've done, you hear?"

With that Caroline took a deep breath. She could tell by the look on Paul's face that he had an inclination of what was to come. He had been in similar situations with her before, but this time it was different. Caroline wasn't shouting, screaming or crying and that made him feel quite uneasy. She closed the file of paperwork and put it to one side, leaving just one piece of paper with a few figures written on it in front of her. This was a Caroline that Paul was not used to seeing. He felt scared and for the first time in his life he had not prepared himself with excuses.

"So, Paul, after receiving a letter from the bank today I had a meeting with the Assistant Manager. He was very helpful and explained all that needs to be done. With the information he gave me and the work I've being doing here, this is what's going to happen. We're going to sell the house. We'll probably get between £200,000 and £230,000 for it, and from that we'll be able to pay back the £62,000 we owe the bank. I need to come away with around £150,000 and what's left will be yours. By the way, all divorce fees will be coming out of your share."

Caroline stood up, walked to the kitchen,

poured herself a glass of wine and started to cook dinner. She was shaking like a leaf as inside her heart was broken, but she had to stay strong. There was no going back, listening to excuse after excuse. There had been 20 years of excuses and she just knew that if Paul continued with his gambling addiction, they would end up with nothing.

About half an hour passed and Paul came into the kitchen. Caroline had drunk the best part of a bottle of wine. As their eyes met, both of them could see that the other had been crying. Caroline was grieving for a marriage that had suddenly died and Paul was crying for the most important thing in his life.

"I love you so much, Paul, and I always will, but I just can't take any more of this. I don't even want to know how all this happened, whether it's betting on the horses, football or at the casino. I'm really not interested how you've lost so much of our money. I just need to start again without the stress and the worry of knowing if I can afford my bills and have a roof over my head. Enough is enough, Paul. You've broken me for once and for all. There are no more chances. I'm so sorry."

"I've no excuses, Caroline, but we can work this out together. I will get it sorted. Things can get back to normal."

"Normal, Paul! What's normal is you betting on anything that moves. No, this time it's over."

Chapter 3

"I know you said you didn't want anything to eat, but I've made you a pasty as I know how much you love them and there's also a jam sponge cake which you can take with you."

"Mum, I've really not got time. It's just a quick in and out I'm afraid, but we do need to sit down as I've got something I need to tell you."

"Oh, Paul, what's wrong? I've never seen you look so tired and anxious before? Is everyone alright?"

"There's no easy way of telling you this, Mum, and it's not something I ever thought would happen, but Caroline and I are splitting up. No one else is involved. Neither of us has met anyone else. Oh, Mum, I'm so sorry. You don't deserve this, please forgive me."

Sandra sat there dazed. Never in a million years did she think this would happen. Throughout all the years Paul and Caroline had been together, she was always amazed how they still seemed to still be like a couple of love struck teenagers. What could have happened for the marriage to end? Surely something could be resolved, and if no one else was involved whatever had gone wrong?"

"Paul, I don't understand. Don't you love each other anymore?"

"We love each other as much today as we've always done. Love isn't the problem."

"So what is the problem, Paul?"

Paul was sobbing and Sandra felt completely in shock, unable to think straight. Had she missed something? They sat there for what seemed hours, but could only have been minutes.

"I've blown it, Mum, messed everything up again. I should have learnt my lesson years ago. Caroline has forgiven me so many times, but this time it's the end. I can't win her round and I can't blame her. It's not just our own lives I've messed up. It's yours too as I know how much you love both of us and you don't deserve to be unhappy. I'm truly sorry, Mum."

"But, Paul, what have you done? If there's no one else involved, whatever is it?"

"I've been betting on the horses and it's got so out of hand that now we need to sell the house and pay the bank back the money I've borrowed. I really don't know how it's got this bad. I just kept thinking 'One big win and I'll be sorted.' It's all a mess and Caroline won't stand for it anymore. She says she wants out and to start afresh. Oh, Mum, I'm so sorry. Neither of us want you to worry. Things will be alright, but I need to go to work now. I'll pop in again tomorrow. I love you lots and so does Caroline, but I need to go."

Sandra always knew that Paul had a gambling problem, but wasn't aware how bad it actually was. What could she do to help? She knew that Paul and Caroline loved each other and therefore there was hope for their marriage. She resolved to concentrate on there still being a future for Paul and Caroline, although they didn't know it themselves.

Over the following months Sandra and Caroline still met up to go shopping and to the cinema. Paul still popped in for his lunch a couple of times a week and life continued in much the same way as it always had. Both Paul and Caroline were surprised how well Sandra was coping with the situation. There were no arguments, tears or shouting, just a couple going through the motions of selling a house and planning a future. It seemed more like a business transaction than the end of the marriage. Once the house was sold, Paul was going to move back to Sandra's and Caroline was going to buy a little house near to her job. They were both planning their new futures.

Chapter 4

It was a cold, dark and wet October night but Caroline had managed it. God knows where she had got the emotional and physical strength from, but this was it, the beginning of a fresh new start. In her mind, she couldn't think further than the bottle of wine she'd just opened to toast her first night in her new home. What lies ahead now? she thought, and What do I do next? Do I even want to be here in this little two up two down? What had drawn her to this little quayside village? Most of the houses here in Saltmarsh Quay were holiday lets and second homes.

The one thing she did know was that the future was not going to be an easy ride. Most of the money she had received from her divorce settlement had been ploughed into buying the cottage, none of the furniture from her old house would fit into it and she could barely afford for anyone to decorate her new home to her previous standards. One glass of wine and that was it. Caroline was tired and off to bed, or rather a single mattress on the floor! Tomorrow, things would begin to look better.

Caroline slept well. She couldn't believe how well. In fact, she hadn't slept so soundly for years as it was nearly nine o'clock when she came down the stairs to pick up her mail from the mat the next morning. She had hardly been in her new home for one day – were bills starting to arrive already? However, as she picked her letters up, she noticed they had neither names nor stamps on them. They were all 'Welcome to Your New Home' cards. Caroline was amazed, overwhelmed at how kind people were. Here were complete strangers wishing her well. What a lovely thing for neighbours to do!

As the day continued, Caroline began the task of cleaning her old fisherman's cottage, but had to keep stopping as people knocked on the door with little gifts – flowers, cakes, wine, even plants for the garden. As much as she wanted to get everything done immediately, it was nice to meet the villagers, find out what was going on and who was who. Apparently, only a quarter of the homes were occupied for the full week, the other three quarters being rented by holiday makers or belonged to owners from London and the Midlands who only came at weekends.

As always, Caroline knew exactly what she wanted to do with her new home. Her vision was clear – very coastal chic with two light and airy bedrooms and a modern bathroom containing a nice big modern shower rather than a bath. Downstairs she would have loved to extend the kitchen out into the coal sheds and keep the front warm and cosy. Perfect for those winter nights when the wind blows across the quay and all you want to do is snuggle up in front of an open fire. In Caroline's mind, she had everything planned but sadly in reality it was going to take a while to complete.

It was nearly eight o'clock and Caroline was just thinking that she should cook herself something to eat when there was another knock at the door. Perhaps it might be more neighbours, hopefully with a roast dinner on a plate or a Chinese takeaway! She was starving hungry and to be honest she'd had enough work for one day, and so to sit down and chat with another neighbour would be lovely.

"Oh hello, Paul. I wasn't expecting you. Do you want to come in out of the cold?"

"I'm not stopping. I just thought you might need a hand with the heavy things, and I wanted to give you these," he said, handing her a bouquet.

"Thank you, they're beautiful. It's a bit like a florist's in here as the neighbours have been so kind and welcoming. The house is still a bit of a tip, but please come and have a look around."

"Caroline, I'm so sorry it's come to this."

"Enough, Paul, that's all in the past. This is the future and if you want us to remain friends the past has to stay in the past. What's happened is behind us. No more talking about it. We've both moved on."

"Yes, but..."

"No, be quiet, and I'll show you around my new abode. First the easy bit, upstairs."

Caroline explained her plans and Paul agreed it

was a lovely little property as whoever had done the place up had carried out a very good job. The central heating, plumbing and electrics were all fine, all it really needed was Caroline's magic touches with the interior design and soft furnishings. The bathroom was straightforward as all the plumbing was in place, the bath just needed removing, to be replaced with a bright new shower unit. The lounge could do with a coat of fresh lightly coloured paint to brighten it up, but what let the property down was its tiny kitchen. Caroline explained that she would like to knock the coal shed into the kitchen and install a patio door out onto the garden. That would give her plenty of space for a table and sofa at some time in the future.

"You don't dither about, Caroline, wondering how things should be. You see something, get a gut feeling about it, and it's always the right road to go down."

You're a builder, Paul. What do you think? Are the plans for my kitchen feasible? How much work do you think will be involved and how much do you think it might cost me?"

"I think your plans are perfect. I'd get rid of the coal house completely, move the kitchen to the back of the lounge wall and add a big conservatory right across the back. That would be quite straightforward and also cheaper. As I put you in this situation, I could do the building work for you for free, you'd just need to sort out the conservatory."

"Thanks, Paul. I'll bear it all in mind. Would you like a drink?"

"No thanks. I won't intrude any longer. Anyway, it's getting late and I ought to be on my way. Good night, Caroline, and again I'm so sorry."

Paul left and Caroline poured herself a glass of wine. Her life had changed so much in little more than just a couple of months. She still loved Paul, but the last thing she needed in her life was a replacement for him. She wasn't looking for either romance or a relationship. She had her job and a new home to get sorted. This was the start of a new chapter in her life.

As the weeks passed, Caroline thoroughly enjoyed working on the cottage. A local plumber had taken the bath out and replaced it with a large shower cubicle and once that was completed, the upstairs of the cottage was ready for the magical makeover. Caroline was so excited as she has spent weeks ploughing through magazines and looking at Pinterest photos, but there was one slight difference this time. She didn't have Paul to do the decorating and to be honest although she knew he would love to be involved, she didn't want his help. She would make sure she was at work while he was doing the building work.

One lunch time she was chatting about the move to Karen, the housekeeper at the hotel, and how she was adapting to living in the quay when Karen happened to mention that that was where her parents lived.

"What a small world, Karen. Have they lived there long?"

"Only a couple of years. After my dad retired, they wanted to be near the sea and enjoy a quieter life. They love it. I'm sure you'll be very happy there as it's such a friendly place. I'm popping over there after work actually. My mum's ordered some new china and I've collected it for her."

If you like I can drop it off for you. It will save you driving over."

"Oh, would you? It could wait until my day off, but it's been ordered for months and my mum's rather excited about it."

Karen gave Caroline the address, they put the china in the back of Caroline's car and off she went. It was easy to find the pretty cottage from the outside and it was a lot bigger than Caroline's. She wasn't at all envious though as she loved her little two up, two down and once the decorating was complete it would be perfect. Caroline knocked on the door and to her surprise a hunk of a lad a lot younger than herself, answered.

"Oh, I'm sorry. I must have the wrong cottage. I'm looking for Mr and Mrs Lark."

"No, you've come to the right place. I'm John. Mr and Mrs Lark are my parents. I'm sorry, they're out at the moment. I think it's their history night, although I'm not quite sure as they belong to so many clubs that they're hardly ever in. Can I help you?"

"Yes, I work with Karen and offered to drop off some parcels for your mum. They're a bit heavy. Do you think you could carry them from my car?"

Caroline followed John back into the cottage, and felt quite excited. She hadn't felt like this for years. She was used to male guests at the hotel flirting and chatting her up, but this didn't feel the same. John was handsome, but he didn't realise how attractive that made him.

Thanks for bringing the china. Mum will be over the moon. She's been going on about it for months. I hope you haven't come far out of your way to drop it off though."

"No, not at all. I've just moved here."

I'm the same. I'm between properties as I've just sold mine and I'm looking for something to buy. In the meantime, I've moved back in with my parents. Actually it's the third time I've done this, so they're getting used to it by now. I buy dilapidated houses, do them up and sell them. It's more of a job really."

"How exciting! That would be my perfect job too. Well, not me doing the work, but the designing parts. I'm in the middle of doing up my own little cottage."

"So you have the ideas and your husband does the work?"

"No, I don't have a husband. That's the reason

I've moved here. It's a long story but I've just got divorced. I'm afraid the work is all down to me, although I'm not afraid of it. I'm excited to be doing it all by myself but I don't know whether I'll be saying the same thing after I've attempted the wallpapering."

"I'm sure you'll be fine. The secret to wallpapering is to start with a straight line. Get that bit right and it's a walk in the park, or in our case on the beach. Look, if you need a hand even if it's just to get your first piece up, just ask. I'm at a dead end at the moment until I find somewhere to buy."

Caroline could feel herself blushing. Had she come across as a helpless woman in need of rescuing? She thanked John, said her goodbyes and returned to her cottage where she poured herself a glass of wine. Looking out the window, she remembered how good looking John was, but he was at least ten years younger than her, possibly even fifteen!

Come on, Caroline. Pull yourself together, she thought. You're acting like a little school girl.

Chapter 5

Leo, or Leonardo, as he preferred to be called, was one of Caroline's best friends and also her work colleague. She always said that everyone needed a 'Leonardo' in their life as he'd been there for her throughout the stressful time of going through the divorce and selling the house. Leo loved drama, in fact he was never happier than when something was happening. At one point they contemplated buying a house together, the Will and Grace of Norfolk, but in reality it wouldn't have been a successful idea as despite loving to spend time together, Caroline and Leo both needed their own space.

Leo hadn't yet seen Caroline's cottage as she hadn't wanted him to talk her out of the purchase. He'd been all for her buying a penthouse apartment in the centre of Norwich, so they could both go out looking for men in the trendy wine bars. Finally, Caroline had agreed that Leo could come and stay the night, but his biggest dilemma was what clothes to bring? He didn't do wellies and certainly would never have been seen dead in a fisherman's smock! A knock at the door. Was she ready for this? Caroline knew full well what was coming.

"Oh, darling, you're far too young to live in a place like this. The shop doesn't even sell olives, dear, let alone Prosecco."

"Come in and make yourself at home."

"Oh, darling, what have you done? The whole place is in darkness. I've not seen a single light on. Where the hell have you moved to?"

"Now just shut up, or you won't be invited in."

Caroline showed Leo around and discussed all her plans. Leo was excited, not just for her but it was something they could do together.

"It's such a blank canvas, darling, and the exciting thing is it's nothing like you've had before. I really think we should go beach shabby chic. Not scruffy, but fresh, very New England. Oh, Caroline, when can we start designing? I hope you have a nice hunky decorator to do the work for you."

There's no money left for a hunk and that means only one thing. Paul will be doing the building work ready for a company to install my fabulous conservatory right across the back of the cottage."

"So, if you haven't got a workman, who's going to be doing it all?"

"We are. Well, that's if you want to help your very best friend."

Without too much persuasion, Leo could see that it only needed basic decorating and both he and Caroline could do the interior design and soft furnishings easily. They had a lovely evening and made a list of things that would look good in the cottage. It was exciting and over the next few months they would have a lot of fun working together.

Every spare minute they had at the hotel Caroline and Leo did nothing else but talk about colours of paint, wallpaper, and furniture. The hotel manager had agreed that Caroline could sleep over at the hotel while Paul was doing the building work plus he was going to be at the cottage while the conservatory was being installed. Once that was all completed, the decorating could commence.

A few weeks later Caroline had cleared everything out of the kitchen ready for Paul to get started. By the time she came back, fingers crossed, a new kitchen and all the building work would be finished, and a few weeks after that the conservatory would be installed. Caroline was packing a suitcase in readiness for leaving her little cottage for two weeks, when there was a knock at the door.

"Oh, hello, John. Do come in. What can I do for you?"

"Well, it's not for me, but my mum. I know this is going to sound lazy, but Mum's bought some shoes that she doesn't like anymore, so she wants Karen to take them back for her. I need to drop them off with Karen, but I was wondering if you could do that rather than me having to drive to Norwich. See, I told you I'm being lazy."

"Don't be silly. Of course that's alright. Would you like a drink, but I've only got wine? No beer I'm afraid."

"Wine would be lovely, thank you."

Caroline showed him around and explained her plans for the cottage. He thought it was good but didn't think that adding a conservatory would add much money to the property. However, Caroline explained that it wasn't a money-making project. It was her home, a new future and a fresh start. One glass of wine led to another and then another and Caroline could feel herself flirting a little, as was John. They were obviously attracted to each other and before long they started to kiss. This was something Caroline hadn't experienced in 20 years, but she was excited for here was this hot hunky fella who clearly wanted her, and God she was ready to give it to him.

Three hours later she was on her front doorstep saying goodbye to John and wondering if the evening had actually happened. They had drunk the wine, enjoyed hot sweaty sex, had coffee, and now John had just left. What was all that about? It was just like something from one of the romance books Caroline liked to read. At the end of the day, there was no commitment to undying love for each other. It was all just a bit of fun.

Chapter 6

Caroline's stomach was in knots. She felt excited but nervous at the same time as it was the first occasion in three weeks that she'd been back to the cottage. Paul had spoken to her on the phone most days, keeping her informed as to the progress of the work. He also kept telling her to call in and take a look at how it was all going, but Caroline knew full well that if she did that and loved it, she would be in a vulnerable situation. Paul was part of her past, not the future. Caroline was even surprised at her own strength. Paul was coming round the next day to go over things, but by then the excitement of seeing the improvements to her new cottage would have settled and she would be able to deal with everything perfectly.

Key in hand she opened the front door. Stepping into the cosy lounge nothing had changed. It was just as she had left it, boxes piled high from floor to ceiling.

Well, here goes, she thought, slowly opening the door into her once tiny little kitchen. The sheer expanse of light overwhelmed her, the room was huge, and she began to cry with happiness. Of course she trusted Paul to do a wonderful job as he had an ulterior motive of wanting her back, but the kitchen was just how she imagined it, with a sleek and modern feel. The conservatory made the room so much bigger. It blended in well, and didn't even look like a conservatory. In her mind she could visualise all her furniture in place, but before she could start work on it, all she needed to do was decorate. Everything was coming together perfectly and she felt so happy.

The next morning Caroline was up early. It was the beginning of her five days off work, and Leo was coming to stay for three of them. They were on a mission to thoroughly decorate the cottage and had bought paint and fabrics as well as an old pine table and dresser which just needed Caroline's magic touch to make them look stunning.

There was a knock on the door. Caroline looked at her watch. It wasn't even eight o'clock in the morning. She knew Leo was keen to get started on the transformation, but it wasn't like him to be this early.

"Oh hello, I thought it was Leo."

"Sorry, I was in the area and wanted to know if everything was alright."

"Come in, but I thought you were going to call in later tonight."

"I couldn't wait to see if everything was okay."

"Yes, Paul. It's out of this world. I'm thrilled to bits with everything. You've done such a good job. Thanks so much."

"It's the least I can do."

With that a car pulled up outside and Caroline could hear loud Abba music blaring. She knew Leo had arrived.

"Morning, you two. How exciting is this? Leonardo Interiors at your service, just like the old days. Caroline and myself doing the painting and Paul doing the building work."

"I think you've got it slightly wrong. We are doing the work, but Paul's just about to leave. He'll be back later to go over a few things, so I suggest you unpack your car, get out of your designer clothes and put a paintbrush in your very manicured hand."

"Oh no, darling. I'm strictly on fabric duty. Lead me to the sewing machine and I'll have cushions and curtains made before you can say 'Kelly Hoppen'."

Caroline noticed the look on Paul's face as he walked towards his van. Although she felt terrible, he had brought all this on himself and as much as she loved him there was no way she could go through it all over again. He was a gambling addict and as much as she had tried to help him, he had to help himself first.

"Come on. Let's have a quick coffee and then it's time for action with Leonardo Interiors."

The day flew by. Leo had set up the sewing machine in the lounge and the CD player pumped out 80s disco music. Caroline had given the kitchen a coat of white paint and before they realised it, it was nearly six o'clock in the evening. They had achieved so much and had enjoyed their day working together.

"Right, Leonardo Interiors, that's enough for now. Go and put your glad rags on and I'll take you to the pub for your tea. If you're lucky, I may get us a bottle of wine on the way home. We need to be back by eight as Paul's popping back with his mum to explain how the new kitchen appliances work."

Caroline and Leo found themselves a seat in a cosy little corner of the pub and ordered two chicken and mushroom pies with all the trimmings and two large gin and tonics. Caroline was discussing how she wanted to paint the pine dresser a shade of duck egg blue, when all of a sudden Leo nearly fell off his chair in surprise.

"Sod the dresser, Caroline. Look at what's just walked in. You didn't tell me anyone like that lived here in Saltmarsh Quay."

Caroline turned round to look and instantly recognised John, who was standing at the bar.

"That's John. He's Karen's brother – Karen is the housekeeper at work."

"Are you telling me you know him? Why on earth didn't you mention this before, Caroline?"

At that moment a very tall, glamorous blonde girl walked in, went straight up to John and they kissed. Caroline felt herself shaking, but after all she knew that her evening with John had only been one of hot casual sex and that he was a lot younger than her. The waitress brought over their meals and Caroline noticed John and the blonde girl move to a table around the corner.

"We need to eat this quickly and get back to the cottage. Paul and his mum will be here soon."

"What's got into you, Caroline? There's plenty of time, although I suppose there's no need to hang around now that the lovely view has disappeared."

As they walked back to the cottage Caroline kept telling herself to snap out of it. Her evening with John had been just that – a one-off, and something which would not be repeated. Once back, she opened some wine and they inspected the lounge curtains they had been making earlier.

"I think they need to just come up a couple of inches. What do you think? Pay attention, Caroline, you've not heard a word I've said. To be honest, you've not been yourself since we went to the pub. Is everything alright?"

"I'm fine, Leo. I'm just not in the mood for Paul and Sandra coming over. The quicker we get it over with the better and then we can get back to Leonardo and Carolina Interiors."

"You what? Where did the 'Carolina' bit come from?"

"The same place as Leonardo."

Caroline had missed not seeing Sandra. That was one of the downsides of moving to Saltmarsh Quay but once the cottage was finished, Sandra would be able to come and stay. Time passed by quickly and all thoughts of John had disappeared from Caroline's thoughts. Paul explained how the kitchen appliances worked and they chatted over a glass of wine. It reminded Caroline of all the times they had spent together over the years. Caroline and Leo were both exhausted and soon after Paul and Sandra had left, they called it a night.

"Another busy day tomorrow, Caroline, but first I might just have to have a walk around the quay to see if Karen has any other brothers hidden away."

Every time someone walked by the window, Leo was quick to look outside, not to mention all the times he noticed a white van in the street.

"Caroline, a white van. That can mean only one thing. A workman, a bit of rough."

Over the next month, work on the cottage was gradually completed and Caroline had ticked off all the jobs from her 'to do' list. Both bedrooms had been painted and new curtains and bedding took pride of place. The bathroom looked so much bigger now that the new modern shower replaced the old bath and the lounge was now comfortable and homely. Leo had done an amazing job with the curtains and cushions and she was delighted with how attractive the sofa and armchair looked. Whoever would have dreamed he could upholster? Another string to his bow. However, without a shadow of doubt, the best part of the cottage was the kitchen diner / family room. Caroline and Leo were thrilled with all they had managed to achieve.

"Well, darling, we've done it. We've created something very special. I want to do it all over again. Well, not right away, as I think we need a little rest first. Do you know, Caroline, you've got the best looking cottage in all of Saltmarsh Quay? You should be so proud of yourself."

"No, Leo, I'm proud of us. We've done this together. You've helped create the most beautiful home and I can't thank you enough."

"Now the hard work is over, let the fun begin."

"What do you mean by fun?"

Over the next few hours Leo persuaded Caroline that she had to show the cottage off to everyone in Saltmarsh Quay. A party would be just the answer, but there was just one problem with that – the cottage wasn't big enough for a party. Instead, they decided on an open house day where friends and neighbours could pop in and out, meaning that everyone would be calling in at different times rather than all at once.

A date was set and the guest list put together. Caroline was slightly nervous about it, but Leo was in his element. There was nothing he loved more than being the hostess with the mostest!

Chapter 7

Paul had neither seen nor spoken to Caroline since the night he and his mum had visited the cottage. He really did miss her and was finding it difficult moving on from the fact that he had messed everything up. Life was beginning to get him down. Although he had lots of work to do, it all seemed very mundane and ordinary and he was bored with the younger men who kept talking about their girlfriends. He realised, however, that he was very fortunate to be back living with his mum. Sandra didn't nag him or talk about his problems with Caroline. She just carried on with her motherly duties, cooking him hot meals and making sure his laundry was done. Paul was indeed quite fortunate in that respect.

As for Sandra, she had continued to meet up with Caroline every week in Norwich, either during a lunch break or after one of Caroline's hotel shifts. For them, life carried on in much the same way as always with their shopping and trips to the cinema. One thing they didn't do was discuss Paul and that made their time together special as there were no awkward conversations.

Sandra was pleased to have Paul living with her again, but as the weeks passed by she could see that he was quite depressed and encouraged him to have nights out with the lads. To begin with Paul wasn't overly keen, but eventually he started going out for a pint or two a couple of evenings a week. Sandra was happy about this as she realised that this would be the only way Paul would get over Caroline and move on with his life.

Every year one of the big building suppliers laid on an evening for all the tradesmen who had supported them over the years. Paul always enjoyed this event as it was a great opportunity to catch up with other builders he had known for years. This year, for obvious reasons, he didn't feel so enthusiastic about attending, but as he didn't want to let anyone down he had to go. The function was always held in one of the grand hotels and each year it was slightly different. Food and entertainment was provided for the evening and it was always a wonderful night out.

Paul arrived at the hotel with his employees. Everyone was in a good mood and as they entered the hotel function room they were all handed an envelope. Paul could not believe his eyes when he opened it and saw it contained gambling chips. That was the last thing he wanted. It would be such a test of strength for him as the hotel room had been turned into a casino for the evening.

"Paul, mate. You must be thinking you've died and gone to heaven. This is your perfect night and we don't have to pay. All the chips are free!"

"Actually, Bruce, it's my worst nightmare. I've not bet or gambled on a single thing since the day I moved out of my house. I haven't even bought a lottery ticket. Here, take my chips and have fun. I'm going to the bar."

Paul met a few chaps at the bar who also didn't want to get involved with the casino entertainment, preferring to talk about work or football and they spent the whole evening together there. As he left to get a taxi at the end of the night, Paul looked up to the sky and said to himself, "I've really done it."

It was quite late when he got back to Sandra's, but he made himself a cup of tea and sat in the lounge. He felt so proud of himself, as any other night in his life he would have joined in at the casino and spent the evening gambling. Paul then broke down in tears which led to really heavy sobbing.

"Whatever's the matter, Paul? What's happened? Come on, tell me. We can sort it out. Take some deep breaths and tell me what's happened."

"Mum, I've started to beat it. I can do it. I promise you I'll win. It's not all over."

"What are you taking about, son?"

Paul proceeded to tell Sandra all about the evening. For years he had been saying that he wouldn't bet on anything ever again, only to be back in the betting shops, casinos, or buying scratch cards within a very short time. This time, however, Sandra believed there was light at the end of the tunnel and she was very proud of Paul.

"Mum, this is the start. I didn't ever think I had

it in me, but look, I have. Now I have a goal to aim for. Just watch me. I'm going to win Caroline back. I'm going to do it, Mum. I really am."

Chapter 8

The day of Caroline's party had arrived, and she was beginning to regret the whole thing. How had she allowed herself to be talked into having an all-day party? What would happen if everyone arrived at the same time? Where would they all go? There was no way she would let anyone sit in the bedrooms. The only positive side was that the weather was pleasant, so people could mingle in the garden. The cottage was spotlessly clean and the fridge and freezer were full. It would be a day of just warming up nibbles and using disposable plastic plates and glasses. The 'Shed' as Leo called it, now had a fresh coat of paint and some curtains and the summer house contained all the alcohol they needed. Wine and beer were definitely the order of the day.

Caroline heard a car door close outside. Leo was standing on her front doorstep dressed to the nines.

"Well, good morning, dear! I thought we were just having a little party here. I didn't realise we were off to star in the Disney parade."

"What do you mean, Caroline? I've gone to a lot of effort to look this good. Please remember it's a very important day for both of us. Today could be the day we meet a very rich man from London who'll whisk us away from that reception desk. We could be living in a beautiful London town house during the week and just living here at weekends."

"Oh, shut up, Prince Charming, and come in and help me finish the cleaning."

Caroline explained how stressed she was about the party and how she just wanted to get the day over with. As usual Leo was able to calm her down and assess the situation logically. He pointed out how the day would easily break down into four sections. All the pensioners from Saltmarsh Quay would be the first to arrive as they'd want to leave by lunch time in order to have their Sunday lunch out. Then there would be a few guests who would either be going for a lunch time drink or be on their way back from the pub. The afternoon would attract the families, and therefore they must be prepared for lots of sticky little fingers everywhere and then finally there would be the young ones recovering from a Saturday night out.

Leo was correct as bang on cue half a dozen pensioners arrived. Caroline was so pleased, as they had all been very kind to her the first week she moved in. It was a great start to her open house day. Time flew by with work colleagues calling in and praising the work done to the cottage. Leo was in his element discussing his designs and showing them his double lined curtains. Caroline was just coming in from the garden when she saw Karen and her mum. She didn't know whether to feel relieved or disappointed that they were alone. There was no time to consider that.

"Hi, Karen. Hello, Mrs Lark. It's so good of you to come. Let me get you a drink. Is your husband not with you?"

"No, he's gone fishing with John. You didn't want their big feet traipsing around the place, did you?"

Caroline briefly thought how much she would have liked John and his big feet in her bedroom.

The next group to arrive were those from London who all had second homes on the quay. Caroline had met them several times in the pub at weekends. The men all worked in the finance sector and the wives were PA to Company Directors, but amongst them there was one face she didn't recognise.

"Hello, I'm Caroline. I don't think we've met."

"I'm so sorry. I feel as if I'm gate-crashing your party, but the group said it would be alright."

"Don't worry. It's fine. Help yourselves to drinks. There's wine or beer and if you're a bit cramped there's plenty of room in the garden. By the way, I'm sorry but I didn't catch your name."

"It's George Barnwell-Smith."

Caroline thought he was rather handsome, but very posh with his double-barrelled name. Perhaps he'd been to Oxford. Looking around, the wives were getting so excited over the cottage whilst all the men wanted to do was discuss the exchange rate between the pound and the dollar.

"Caroline, please tell us which interior company

you've used for your cottage. All this must have cost a fortune, the fabrics are stunning. Our cottage is just the same size as this, but the way it's been designed you've so much space. So beachy shabby chic."

"I must interrupt you, ladies. I'm the interior designer and the company is called 'Chic Quayside Living'. It's fresh and new and in a short time everyone will be wanting it."

"Ladies, this is Leo, a very dear friend of mine."

With that Caroline's mobile rang and so she left the very excited women questioning Leo about the sofa covers. The call was from Sandra apologising that she and Paul wouldn't be able to call in as Paul wasn't feeling too well. Caroline felt slightly relieved. As much as she would have liked Sandra to see the finished cottage, it probably would have been awkward having Paul there. As she made her way back to her guests, Caroline felt that someone was staring at her. Turning around, she noticed it was George, but at the same time someone else came through the front door. Leo and the group of chatty wives fell silent and stood there open mouthed as in came John wearing the tightest T-shirt and jeans that she thought Leo was going to faint.

"Hi, John. Thanks for coming. Can I get you a beer? Your mum said you'd gone fishing."

"Yes, we did, but we decided to give it a miss as it was so busy. You look nice, Caroline. I've been meaning to pop back and—"

"Hello, I'm Leo and I'm responsible for creating this beautiful cottage. You're John, Karen's brother, aren't you? We saw you a few weeks back in the pub with your girlfriend. Isn't she with you today?"

"Leo, perhaps you could get John a drink. I just need to speak to these people before they leave."

For some strange reason John didn't stay very long and the rest of the party flowed nicely. The London group said their goodbyes as most of them were travelling back to the capital ready for another stressful week. By eight o'clock only Caroline and Leo were left and so they began the task of tidying up after their guests.

"Why don't I open another bottle of wine while it's still so nice out here? You can go and sit out on the patio. You're not driving and we're both off work tomorrow, so it will make a lovely end to the day. You can tell me all about the London wives and their many questions."

"Yes, and you, the newly divorced single lady, can tell me what's gone on with Mr Tight Jeans. I know something has and you should have told me about it before."

Caroline told Leo the story of how she met John and what had happened. Leo was flabbergasted.

"So, will it happen again? Do you want more from Mr Tight Jeans?"

"Who knows? It might, but I'm not holding my

breath. I think I was just one of many here in Saltmarsh Quay that have had 'the John welcome'."

"I'm moving here right now. I want the John welcome."

They laughed and drank wine and talked about the lovely day they'd had. Caroline was so happy to have moved to Saltmarsh Quay and was surprised that after such a short period of time she had managed to feel at home. Life was beginning to sort itself out and she felt very happy.

Chapter 9

Caroline and Leo were both up early the next day as they wanted to get everything cleared up from the night before and then go for a nice long walk followed by a pub lunch. Leo was just getting out of the shower when his mobile rang and Caroline had just finished emptying the dishwasher when her mobile rang at exactly the same time. After about ten minutes they both started screaming with excitement and running towards each other.

"You'll never guess who that was! I can't believe it."

"No, my news is far more exciting."

When they had both calmed down, they explained to each other who their calls were from. Caroline told Leo that her call was from George thanking her for a lovely Sunday.

"George? Who's George?"

"He's the chap who came with the group from London. He apologised for just turning up without being invited, but said he'd had a lovely time and he'd like to take me out to dinner when he's next in Norfolk as a thank you."

"You don't mean that boring looking chap, who if you don't mind me saying looked like a fifty-year-old virgin, do you?" Oh, Caroline, I thought you had some exciting news. It's a good job my call was because it's going to blow your mind with excitement. It's what we've both been dreaming of.

Well, it's been my dream – not the dream about Mr Tight Jeans, but one which I've been having for years."

Leo continued by telling Caroline that his call had been from Charlotte, one of the London ladies. Apparently, she had loved Caroline's cottage so much that she wanted them both to renovate her cottage in the same quayside chic style and wanted to know how much it would cost and when they could start.

"Now, Mr Designer, let me get this right, and please correct me if I'm wrong. You've led Charlotte to believe we're a team of interior designers who do this for a living rather than two hotel receptionists. The reason you helped me with my cottage was because I was short of money and you love to experiment with soft furnishings. What did Charlotte say when you told her the truth?"

"I told her I didn't think we'd be able to take on the project as we're so busy. I thought she'd take no for an answer..."

"But... and somehow I feel this is going to be a very big but."

"Please don't be mad with me, Caroline. I didn't exactly mention that we don't do this for a living. Charlotte did say that she would be willing to pay extra to get the project started as soon as possible."

"You need to call her back and say that there's been a terrible mistake, and if you don't do it I certainly will. The last thing I need is to get a bad name for myself here in Saltmarsh Quay."

"Excuse me, Caroline, the only bad name you'll get is if people find out about you and Mr Tight Jeans. First there was Paul, then John and now there's a George. You only need a Ringo and you'll have the full set."

Two weekends later Caroline and Leo were sitting round Charlotte's kitchen table discussing paint colours for the cottage makeover. Leo had cleared the air with Charlotte and taken Caroline's advice, but he was right, Charlotte was not one to take no for an answer. Her solution was that Leo and Caroline could design and project manage her cottage makeover, but they would need to employ a builder and decorator to do the major renovations. Problem solved!

"I don't want a mirror image of your cottage, Caroline, but I would like the same style and textures. I'm so excited about the whole thing. Having the house in London refurbished was so stressful, as the designer had an image in mind and basically, I had to like it whether I wanted it or not. Later I discovered that was because she wanted to update her portfolio for a bigger project. Sorry, I've been rambling. Tell me your ideas for my cottage and please be honest if you don't think any of my ideas would work out well."

Caroline went on to explain how pleased they were to be carrying out the project and since looking at the cottage the previous week they were both excited about the plans. The upstairs was very straightforward as the family bathroom was new and fresh and wouldn't need any renovations. The three bedrooms would benefit from the dark beams being painted white as this would lift the ceilings and also make the room look larger.

The majority of the work would be downstairs. Caroline and Leo suggested that the whole of the ground floor level be open plan and split into zones by the addition of rugs and extra lighting with bi-fold doors leading out onto the patio. Leo showed Charlotte mood boards for fabrics and paint and also suggested that the kitchen units and door should be saved and moved to a side wall which would help to improve the flow of the room.

"I'm super excited and so pleased you're going to take this job on. It's going to look fabulous. Oh, by the way, have you found a company to do the construction work and have you managed to see any work they've done in the past?"

"Yes, a very good friend of Caroline's is going to be doing the building work. She's more than happy with the way John performs, aren't you, Caroline?"

Caroline could have hit Leo over the head with one of his mood boards, but this was a professional meeting and that would have to wait until later. Despite Leo's sarcasm she had seen John's work as he had modernised his parent's house before they had moved in. They discussed the rate of pay with John and surprisingly it didn't take much persuasion for him to agree to do the required construction work on Charlotte's cottage.

A time schedule was set. Charlotte and her husband would not need to stay at the cottage for a month to six weeks and she gave them the go ahead to begin work. One thing Caroline hadn't told Leo two nights previously when discussing money with John was that they had ended up sleeping together again. Well, not actually sleeping. They'd had hot sweaty sex on the kitchen floor. It was very good as this time neither of them were at all nervous. They both knew what they wanted. Job done!

Chapter 10

After several meetings with John – a few of which Caroline avoided going to – leaving everything up to Leo, time schedules were agreed upon and the first phase of the project, involving removing a ground floor wall and installing a steel beam, was about to begin. The upstairs could then be blocked off and Caroline could begin decorating the bedrooms. Leo had taken all the measurements for blinds and curtains and had set up a work room in his flat. There was a lot of work to do, but he was so excited about the project. They were both surprised that Charlotte wasn't coming to see how things were getting on and didn't need any updates. She seemed to have so much faith and confidence in Leo and Caroline's work that she would just arrive on the completion date and take over her newly renovated cottage.

They were now about a third of the way through the project, the wall had been removed, the installation of the steel beam was completed and the downstairs had been fully plastered. John was away for a few days and they had the cottage to themselves. Leo hadn't seen it for a few weeks, so he had a real surprise when he walked through the front door.

"Oh my God, it's huge! This room's going to be fabulous with the light coming right through the bi-fold doors. Come on, Caroline, show me the upstairs."

Caroline had made progress with the bedrooms, spending hours painting the old dark beams white. As she had predicted, it would lift the rooms. Now they could add their magic to the three blank white boxes before them. In the master bedroom they wanted to make a feature wall. Leo had brought some wallpaper samples with him. The most obvious thing to do was create the feature wall behind the bed, but they wanted this project to be different and rather quirky. As the room was empty, they marked out the size of the bed with newspapers and moved it around the room.

"Do you know, I think if the bed stays quite close to that wall, we'd have enough space for a nice armchair in front of the window."

"Yes, Caroline, that would be good, but where would the wardrobes go?"

"It's only a weekend home, so one wardrobe would be enough and then that beautiful duck egg blue paper could go in the alcove with the chair and a little table beside it. It would be a perfect place for Charlotte to escape to with her book."

They spent the rest of the morning going from one room to the next planning their designs. Downstairs they marked out the different zones with masking tape. The room needed to serve two purposes. When Charlotte and her husband were there alone it needed to be a cosy room, and when they were entertaining it needed to accommodate lots of people without feeling cramped. By the end of the day Leo and Caroline were very pleased with their achievements as they had also given two of the bedrooms a further coat of paint.

Back at the cottage, over a bottle of wine, they went through the facts and figures making sure they didn't exceed Charlotte's budget for the work. They still needed to buy furniture, pictures and rugs, but with careful Internet research they were sure they could purchase them at a good price.

"The big question you're dying to ask, Leo, is how much money will we make out of this. You won't believe it, but I think once John and the plasterer have been paid, we'll be left with nearly three thousand pounds. That's not bad for six weeks' work."

They spent the rest of the evening browsing the Internet for everything from rugs to garden plant pots, just like two children let loose in a sweet shop.

"Caroline, why is it we've not had any of those disasters where the budget goes completely overboard, like you see on the TV makeover programmes?"

"I don't know. Probably because we've planned every stage of the project and costed out what we've needed to purchase. We've known that it all had to add up as it isn't our own home we're renovating now."

Over the next few weeks John refitted the

kitchen and an electrician completed the lighting. After email negotiation with Charlotte they agreed that the whole of the downstairs would be painted white with splashes of colour in the fabrics and paintings. They were now on the homeward leg of the project.

As the same time as all this was taking place, Caroline accepted George's dinner offer. She was more than happy and not nervous about the date in the slightest as she didn't find George attractive. It would just be an opportunity to get to know someone else from Saltmarsh Quay. George had agreed to pick Caroline up at seven o'clock and to her surprise they were going to the Saltmarsh Cliff Hotel rather than the local pub. Caroline was pleased she had made the effort to dress up. The five-star restaurant at the hotel had the most stunning views out to sea, and the food was to die for.

"Thank you so much, George. This is very kind of you, but I would have been more than happy with the local pub."

"It's lovely here. Caroline. Through coming to this hotel, I fell in love with Saltmarsh Quay. You're so lucky to live here seven days a week. I'd love to wake up here every day and not in smoky old London. Yes, London does have a lot going for it and it's a very exciting place when you're young, but the older you get the more you appreciate peace and quiet, not to mention fresh clean air.

Anyway, that's enough about me. Tell me all about yourself. What brought you to this stunning part of the country?"

Caroline began to talk about her life, explaining to George all about her problems with Paul. She felt totally at ease chatting to him as he was a gentle man and she could tell he was really listening to all she was saying instead of just saying yes and no at the right time.

"It's obvious that you still love Paul and it's such a massive shame you were unable to resolve all your problems."

"Just before moving here I would have agreed that I was still in love with Paul, but as the weeks and months have passed, I'd now say that I love him, but I'm not in love with him, if that makes sense? That's enough about me, George. All I know about you is that you live and work in London and come here for a weekend now and then. What do you do in London? I presume you're in finance like the rest of the London group."

As the evening progressed and they worked their way through the beautiful three course meal and a bottle of wine, George spoke about his past. Yes, he was connected to finance as he advised companies on investments both in the UK and overseas. He had spent his early life in Wiltshire before going to boarding school and then university and considered it all rather uninteresting.

"Basically, Caroline, I've had a very boring life and I didn't even realise that until I bought my little cottage here on the quay. Tell me, how can such a quiet place with very few people bring me such pleasure and make me feel as if I've wasted my life ensuring other people had plenty of money to enjoy theirs?"

"You've realised it now because someone or something in the past has stopped you from being the person you really wanted to be. Now that you've come here and contemplated everything, I don't think you were aware how unhappy you actually were."

George and Caroline sat looking out at the lights at sea. There were a couple of fishing boats way off out in the distance. Caroline smiled to herself. The two men she had spent time with in the last few weeks could not be more different to each other. George just appeared to be interested in chatting and enjoying her company whereas John couldn't wait to rip her clothes off and have rampant sex with her.

"What are you smiling about, Caroline? Was it something I said?"

"No, I was also reflecting on life and it made me smile."

As they had both been drinking, George decided to phone for a taxi to take them home, but Caroline suggested they walk back down to the quay."

"It's not too cold and will only take about twenty

minutes. It will do us the world of good to walk. Come on, George, let's throw caution to the wind."

They chatted and giggled all the way back to Caroline's cottage. She asked him to come in for a coffee, but he declined the offer, which Caroline thought was rather strange.

"Perhaps we could do this again sometime? I'm coming back for a whole fortnight next week and that will be the first time I've ever done that. No driving and no work! I'm so looking forward to it."

"Well, George, that's a date! I'll cook us some dinner and you'll have a holiday to remember."

George agreed that would be very nice and he would look forward to it. They said goodnight and Caroline gave him a little kiss on the cheek. He was slightly shocked but thanked her for a lovely evening. As she closed the door behind her, she thought: What a gentleman, but what I really mean is that he's a very gentle man.

During the following week, John had completed the kitchen and the new electrics were all finished. The only job left for John was tiling the massive floor but this had been delayed as Caroline and Leo couldn't agree on which tiles to use. This was the first time they had disagreed on anything on the project. Caroline realised that the tiling needed to be practical, something which didn't show any dirt as the last thing Charlotte would want to do on her return to Norfolk was to spend the weekend cleaning. However, Leo preferred to add a little bit of bling, so eventually they compromised on a practical floor with a modern twist.

With the floor done, everyone was happy. John had finished all his work and only the last magical touches needed finalising. They were all excited as the furniture had been styled in a shabby chic fashion and Leo had completed the curtains and cushions. Caroline was going to pay John his final payment and secretly hoping for something in return. She had made quite a bit of effort in her appearance and when he arrived she offered him a beer. He refused, saying that a cup of tea would be fine. He didn't have that twinkle in his eyes. He was friendly, but not in an excited way and Caroline couldn't help but feel disappointed.

"John, thanks again for all the hard work you've put in here. We could never have done it without you."

"I've enjoyed it, and if ever you decide to do it again, count me in."

"Oh, I don't think it will ever happen again. It would be great, but sadly I think it's just a one off."

John left, and Caroline thought: Okay, you can't win them all. Perhaps it was for the best.

It was going to be a busy week with only nine days before the keys were to be handed back to Charlotte. The cottage needed a real deep clean and all the furniture had to be put back in place, dressed and looking its very best, plus Caroline had to entertain George. There was still something about him that she couldn't fathom out. Despite talking about his life, he hadn't really mentioned either himself or his family. It all seemed quite strange.

"Welcome back to my little cottage, George. You must be so excited to be spending two weeks in Saltmarsh Quay. Let me take your coat and get you a drink. Do take a seat."

"Thank you. Yes, it will be like a rehearsal for when I retire and live here permanently."

"You've got years before that happens."

Caroline had cooked a traditional cottage pie followed by apple pie and custard and they enjoyed a lovely evening. George was keen to hear all about Charlotte's cottage and said he couldn't wait to see it. He explained his plans for the next two weeks and that he would walk the coastal path each day and then catch the little coast hopper bus. Hopefully, over the fortnight he would get to see quite a bit of Norfolk. As the evening continued, Caroline couldn't help but notice that George hadn't talked about any of his friends or family, but how could she approach the subject? With that the phone rang. It was Charlotte telling her what time they would be arriving on Friday evening and how excited she was to see her cottage.

"That was Charlotte. Did you know her and her husband, Clifford, before you bought your place here?"

George explained that he and Clifford were at

boarding school together and had met each other at business events over the years. Charlotte and Clifford were the reason why George had moved to Saltmarsh Quay as he stayed at the hotel when they were having a party one weekend.

"Caroline, may I tell you something? You've been most kind to me, so I think it's best that I tell you about my family and my hideous childhood."

"No, George, you don't have to explain anything to me. Your private life is your own business."

"I would like to."

George explained that he was an only child and had been sent to boarding school at five years old. He had hated it, but his way of coping was to just do as he was told. Sadly, his mother had passed away when he was ten years old, his father had remarried a year later and George had then felt as if he was in the way.

"Is your father still alive?"

"Oh yes, very much alive and very active. My stepmother passed away a couple of years ago and as yet I don't think he's replaced her."

"Don't you see much of him, George? Sorry to ask so many questions, but aren't you close as a family?"

"That's fine. I will explain, Caroline. Not many people know this, but my father is the Earl of Coolten."

Oh my God, you could have knocked Caroline off her seat. The Earl of Coolten was one of the old school rich men, old money breeding, and always in the press for having younger lady friends on his arm. Caroline was shocked as George explained that in the last 20 years they had only spoken three or four times. Neither had any time or love for the other and that's the way it would stay.

"Subject closed, Caroline. Now tell me all about your next project. Will it be here on the quay?"

"There'll be no more projects, George. This one was just a little bit of luck which fell into our laps, but Leo's all for branching out, throwing in our jobs and becoming full time interior designers."

"That sounds exciting. He's a fun chap and he gave the impression that he did interior design for a living. Tell me more about him. He's certainly the life and soul of the party. Have you known each other long?"

Caroline noticed how quickly George had manipulated the conversation away from his father and himself, and spent the next hour recalling stories of all the fun times that she and Leo had experienced over the past 20 years. It had been a nice evening and a great start to George's holiday and they agreed to catch up for a drink or a meal during his fortnight at Saltmarsh Quay.

Lying in bed that night, Caroline felt that she understood George a bit better, but there was still something missing. Although it was none of her business, perhaps it was something she could lend a helping hand to.

Chapter 11

It was the day of the grand reveal. Both Caroline and Leo had taken the day off work although Charlotte and Clifford weren't due to arrive at the cottage until early evening. On his way from Norwich Leo had bought enough flowers to open a florist's shop, as well as a stock of candles. He and Caroline were rather apprehensive. Although they loved the look they'd created, it wasn't their property. Would everything be practical for Charlotte and Clifford? Even though it was only a holiday home, it still needed to be a functional home.

"Caroline, do you think we should bake some bread to give the cottage a lovely homely smell."

"Don't be silly. It's not our home. We've done everything contained in the brief and come in both on budget and on time. There's nothing else we can do apart from wait."

They chatted together while waiting for Charlotte and Clifford as Leo was interested to hear whether Caroline and John had been rolling around on the kitchen floor together lately. He was disappointed to hear that they hadn't and jokingly suggested that he should try his luck. Caroline also discussed her dates with George and that he was a nice man although very shy.

"But, darling, he's so old fashioned. His clothes look like they came from the forties. He's got a fair few decades to catch up on. Have you rolled on the kitchen floor with him yet?"

"Don't be so horrible, Leo. No, I haven't and neither do I intend to. He's just a lovely man who just needs a friend to help him, how can I put it ... come alive. Yes, that's it. He just needs an introduction to this modern and exciting world we live in. He needs someone to show him how to have some fun."

"As well as fun, darling, he needs a good stylist and hairdresser. Perhaps after we hand this place over to Charlotte, George could become your next project."

"Oh no, not my project, but I do know someone. You could really help George. Now come on, one final wipe of the windowsills and a plump of the cushions and our work here is done."

Dead on cue a car pulled up outside and Charlotte emerged before turning off the car's engine.

"It seems really weird opening your front door to you. It should be the other way around."

"Come on, come on, let me in. I'm so excited! I just know I'm going to love it. Sorry, we're both going to love it."

"We'll stay here. You just go and explore."

"No, please come and show us everything you've done."

This is where Leo could come into his own as a real showman. Charlotte and Clifford were astounded to see how much lighter the cottage was. Even though it was the same kitchen, it now looked so bespoke and the painted furniture was definitely a trade mark style. The new wood burner, which seemed to fill the room, was such a stunning feature that helped to pull the whole room together.

"I love the modern floor tiles. They really lift the room."

"Thank you. Did you hear that, Caroline? I didn't hear the word 'practical' at all. Charlotte said it was modern."

"Alright, Leo, you win, but the floor tiles are easy to keep clean."

Leo left the master bedroom until last as this was the room they hoped would really show off their impeccable style and taste.

Charlotte and Clifford were amazed. They couldn't believe how big the room now looked just by whitening the beams and the chair set in front of the window was perfect.

"Right, you two. When can you make a start on our London home? I'm only joking for the time being, that is. I'm really surprised that you both don't do this for a living. Your talents are so wasted."

Back at Caroline's and over a pizza and quite a few glasses of wine, everyone was on a high. There was nothing they would want to change about the cottage. It could be summed up by just one word –

success!

The following morning, both with sore heads and back down to earth, they knew it was all over. Their little project had come to an end and as much as they both would have loved doing it again, they knew it wasn't going to happen. Leo had decided to stay with Caroline until Monday morning and she knew the reason why. Charlotte would be showing her home off to anyone who was willing to look at it and Leo wanted to walk around Saltmarsh Quay calling himself Leonardo and taking all the praise. However, Caroline was more than happy to let Leo do this.

On the way to the shop Caroline bumped into George. He had already heard what a great success the cottage was and had been invited to Sunday lunch. Caroline was pleased to see him and invited him for supper. George accepted her offer and carried on with his day exploring every nook and cranny on the coastal path. Back at the cottage Caroline felt proud of herself. She glanced in the mirror and said, "Project number two, here we go."

"Sorry, darling? What did you say? Number two?"

"Oh, never mind, Leo. I was only talking to myself."

They spent a quiet afternoon together. Leo wasn't happy that Caroline had invited George over for dinner but supposed that it could be fun. He thought they could talk about vintage cars, not that he knew anything about cars at all.

"I just need to give the hotel a quick ring to make sure everything's alright. Hi, Helen…"

George arrived punctually at seven o'clock and poured all three of them a drink."

"Darling, what are you drinking? Is that orange juice? I'm shocked! It's a Saturday night and no wine?"

"I'll have some soon. I just fancy this first."

"All the years' I've known you and I can't believe how you still manage to keep amazing me."

With that the phone rang. Caroline answered, "Oh dear, right away. Give me half an hour."

"What's that all about?"

"Oh dear, there's a problem with the computer system at the hotel and I need to pop in and sort it out. It shouldn't take long. I'm so sorry, George, but Leo will entertain you while I'm away. The fish pie is nearly ready. Have a lovely evening."

Before either of them could say a word, Caroline had disappeared, thinking to herself: Hopefully project two will be completed.

To be honest, she wasn't really lying, although it was possibly a little white lie. She did go to the hotel and got on with a few hours' worth of paperwork and also sent Leo a text to explain that as she was due to start an early shift the next day she would be staying there overnight. Leo returned her text with a tick, but Caroline wasn't quite sure what that meant.

Back at the cottage Leo served up the fish pie and seemed to be pouring a lot of wine. The conversation turned to all the countries they had visited and Leo realised that George wasn't as boring as he had first thought. George had travelled the world, which Leo found incredibly interesting. As the evening went on they were really getting on well. George was feeling hot, so he took off his jumper and as it went up over his head his shirt rose up and Leo noticed what a good body he had. It got to about one o'clock and neither of them were drunk, just a little merry. All of a sudden George stood up, walked towards Leo and kissed him on the cheek.

"Would you like to come home with me tonight, Leo?"

Chapter 12

Over the next couple of weeks, people on the quay stopped Caroline to tell her how nice Charlotte and Clifford's cottage looked. There didn't seem to be a single person in Saltmarsh Quay who hadn't been shown around. Caroline began to get the impression everyone thought she was lending her services for free as all she heard was "I'd love you to come and give me a few ideas. I'm good with a sewing machine. Oh, you do have an eye for that." One or two people asked her whether she'd make them some cushions and so she passed on Leo's phone number to them.

Talking of Leo, neither of them had mentioned the night with George. It was so unlike Leo not to discuss his life with Caroline, but after all, she had kept John a secret for a few weeks. John had been seen in the pub with yet another young lady on his arm, the only difference this time was that both his parents were there. Caroline wasn't bothered. She was pleased for John, but did think to herself that the girl he was with was very lucky.

Life was very much the same for the next few weeks. Caroline continued to meet up with Sandra and neither of them mentioned Paul. Work was going well and Caroline was enjoying life in her cottage. Although her path crossed with Leo's from time to time, she wasn't seeing as much of him as he'd changed his shifts at the hotel, preferring to work long days and then take three or four days off. Caroline didn't know what Leo was doing with his time off, but sensed that it involved George.

***

Leo was sitting on a train for what seemed to be hours. He felt rather nervous which wasn't really like him. He'd met George twice over the past few weeks; first George had stayed in his flat and the second time they had both gone to Brighton for a few days. This time was going to be different as Leo was travelling to George's home in Central London. As the train pulled into the station Leo knew he had to transform himself into the happy carefree character he had created over the years – the one that George seemed to like!

"Would you like to go for something to eat or visit the sights?"

"I've seen the sights of London many times over forty years. Let's go to your home instead."

"Are you sure? It's really not anything special. I've had it for twenty years and in all that time I've never decorated or done anything at all with it. It's got the same wallpaper up as the day I moved in. You'll be shocked."

"It's not your home I've come all this way to see, but I'm sure it will be lovely."

Leo and George got a taxi and as Leo stared out of the window at the busy streets he thought: Yes, I have come to see George and get to know him better, but I do hope he lives somewhere nice, not just above a takeaway shop.

George and Leo chatted as they travelled and Leo was excited that George kept touching him. Knowing that someone found him attractive was a good feeling, as was the thought of feeling wanted.

As the taxi pulled up, Leo noticed they were at a crossroads with four streets leading into different directions. While George was paying the cab driver, he wondered if they'd have to walk the rest of the way. It all looked rather strange.

"Come on, Leo. It's just down here."

Leo followed George down the street. Bloody hell, he thought, this looks just like something out of 'My Fair Lady'. Oh, my God, don't say he lives here!

Two hours later George needed to attend to some emails and Leo said that he had to phone the hotel as he had forgotten to tell Caroline something about a guest who was checking in. George went into his study and Leo stayed in the morning room.

"Caroline, why, oh why, didn't you tell me where he lived? You could have warned me."

"I presume you mean George? I've no idea where he lives, apart from in London."

"Are you serious? I hope you're sitting down as I've been here two hours and my legs are still shaking like jelly. George lives in a town house! Yes, a Belgravia town house with three floors and a library. I'm talking to you from the bloody morning room. It must be worth millions."

George knocked on the door. "Hello, George, you don't need to knock. It's your home. Come in. It's nothing private. That's all, Caroline, could you just make sure they're not feather pillows and they want to dine at 7.45pm. Sorry, I didn't write it down for you. Have a lovely shift. Bye."

They spent a lovely afternoon and evening together with quite a bit of it spent in bed. It had been years since anyone had wanted him in that way and to be honest he couldn't remember the last time he had been cuddled.

"Good morning. Here's a cup of tea. I've not brought any breakfast up. I'm not a very good host, I'm sorry."

"Don't be sorry. I can't remember when I last had a cup of tea in bed. Oh yes, when we were in Brighton."

"Now what would you like to do today? I'm afraid I'm not very good at this entertainment lark. Perhaps it's because I've never done it before."

For a start you can stop apologising for everything. We'll have a lovely day out, but if you don't mind there is something I'd like to do. Please don't take this the wrong way, but George you dress as if you're eighty and you're only in your forties. Would you mind if I take you shopping and modernise you a little?"

"Is modernise a real word?"

"Oh, I'm sorry. It's not that I want to change you as a person, but I just want you to look more how you should look for your age."

George laughed and said that one of his secretaries had been saying the same for years. "Of course you can bring me into the twenty-first century on one condition and that's as a thank you, I'll take you for afternoon tea at the Ritz."

"The Ritz! Oh, no, George. There's no need for that. I've not come prepared."

"You don't need to be prepared. All you need to do is eat cake, drink tea and be yourself, Leo."

The first stop of the day was to a Toni and Guy hair salon where a lovely girl called Lucy with a fabulous sense of humour, took instructions from Leo.

"All I need you to do is take twenty years off him. He needs to go from William Pitt to Brad Pitt."

"Who's William Pitt? I know who Brad is."

"Oh, darling, William Pitt was Prime Minister hundreds of years ago."

"Oh, you are funny. I'll see what I can do. Do you agree with all this, George? It is your hair I'm going to be cutting and you can always refuse."

"Lucy, you can do whatever you like. Whatever you do to my hair won't make the slightest difference to how happy I'm feeling right now. I'll tell you a secret – I've never been this happy in all my life."

The haircut was the start of a brilliant day. George had such patience trying on clothes, everything from jackets, trousers and even jeans, which he'd never owned or worn in his life. They looked at all the styles except those in tartan or corduroy. "Goodbye hunting lodge and hello wine bar" was the motto for the day, finished with tea at The Ritz as promised.

"You look so handsome, George. I think I might have done too good a job as now I'm feeling fat and haggard sitting next to you. Please could you pass the clotted cream?"

***

While Leo was having fun in London, Caroline was having an evening at the cinema with Sandra. First, they were going to have a quick pizza and then they were off to see a girly film. Caroline filled Sandra in on Leo's news and they both agreed that it was time he found someone to settle down with.

"Your turn next, Caroline. Surely there's a nice eligible gentleman in Saltmarsh Quay."

"It's the last thing on my mind, I can tell you. I've got my busy job and my lovely new home. What do I need a man for?"

It was just what Sandra wanted to hear. There was a light at the end of the tunnel and now that Paul was feeling better with himself and had finally beaten his gambling habit, she had to believe him.

After all, Sandra was his mother and who else was there to support him?

Chapter 13

As the weeks passed, Leo spent more and more time with George in London as well as in Saltmarsh Quay. Caroline was very happy for both of them, although she did miss Leo's company. They had invited her to join them on shopping trips and going out to dinner, but Caroline always declined as she didn't wish to be a gooseberry. However, one weekend the opportunity arose for the perfect get together. Sandra was coming to stay with her for a few days and it just happened to be the same weekend that George was staying in Saltmarsh Quay. Caroline decided to have a little dinner party for the four of them as she knew Sandra would be excited to meet George, and Leo always had her in stiches with his stories and bitchy comments.

Caroline picked Sandra up on the Friday evening after work and they decided to go to the pub for a drink and something to eat. It was quite busy, but they managed to get a table.

"Hello, Caroline."

"Hi, John. How are you? Can I introduce you to my ex mother in law, Sandra? Actually, I must stop saying that. John, this is Sandra, my best friend. Sandra, this is John. He's the chap who did all the hard work on Charlotte's cottage before Leo and myself threw a few cushions around."

"Oh don't put yourself down, Caroline. You designed it. There's no way it would have looked that good if it wasn't for your vision and talent."

"Well, thanks, but I think a lot of it was down to luck."

"Nice to meet you, Sandra. Do have a lovely evening."

"He seems a very nice young man and so very handsome. Looking at him, I bet he's got a girl in every village along the coastal path. He'd only need to flutter those beautiful dark eyelashes and the ladies would fall at his feet."

"Oh, come on, Sandra. Let's order some food."

Sandra sensed Caroline had noticed how good looking John was. As the evening progressed, different people popped by to say hello and there was such a lovely atmosphere in the pub.

"Caroline, you've certainly made the right decision moving here. Everyone's so nice. It reminds me of years ago when life was so much simpler. I'm very envious."

On the way back to the cottage they bumped into Charlotte and Clifford who had just driven up from London for the weekend. After the usual introductions, Charlotte invited them both round for a drink on Saturday lunch time. Sandra was very excited as she wanted to see exactly how Caroline and Leo had styled her cottage.

"I thought I was coming for a quiet weekend and suddenly I've become a social butterfly. How exciting is this, Caroline!"

They were both up early the next morning and

after lots of coffee and crumpets they went for a walk around the quay and a little way along the coastal path. Sandra loved the fact that everything was on their door step and there was no need to drive anywhere. Back at the cottage they had a warming hot chocolate drink and they got ready to go to Charlotte's.

"Caroline, what does one wear to a Saturday lunch drinks party?"

"Don't worry, Sandra. No one dresses up here in Saltmarsh Quay. Just put on something you feel comfortable in."

There were about eight or nine people at the informal lunch get together. Sandra was so impressed with all Caroline had done with the cottage and she could tell that both Charlotte and Clifford were over the moon with the finished look.

"See what Caroline and Leo have done! They've made it perfect for when there's a group here like today. There's plenty of space and everyone can join in on the conversation. Plus, two or three little groups can chat separately and then when it's just the two of us here it feels so cosy. We're so happy with our cottage, I want them to come to London and redesign our main home."

"Yes, they're both very talented. I'm so proud of them both."

"But Sandra you haven't mentioned that you taught both Leo and myself to make cushions and curtains. Yes, Charlotte, everything to do with sewing we've learnt from this lovely lady."

Caroline was hoping that Leo and George would have been there to share the afternoon, but they weren't driving up from London until early evening. She felt as if she were a bit of a fraud taking all the credit, but she was very proud and never in a month of Sundays did she ever believe that she could have managed such a project. The TV makeover programmes only portrayed all the problems.

Back at Caroline's they both put their feet up and had a little snooze. A gammon joint was cooking away in the slow cooker and the pudding only needed to be defrosted from the freezer. It was exactly how weekends should be – eating with friends and family. Later that afternoon, Caroline nipped to the little shop for some more wine and bumped into John on the way back.

"Hi, are you having a nice weekend? I was thinking, perhaps we should get together sometime, if you know what I mean. I think the sooner the better as I won't be around Saltmarsh Quay for too much longer. I've bought a property about eighty miles away, which is a bit too far to commute back to my parents' every night."

"Yes, John, that would be very nice, but I don't think so. Perhaps you should just have a ride on the coast hopper to the next village, because I'm sure you will find someone there."

Caroline was disappointed with herself on two

counts. Firstly, John didn't really deserve to be spoken to like that. It wasn't like her to be so sarcastic and also she would have loved nothing more than to be rolling around with Mr Tight Jeans on top of her. But never say never; who knew what the future might hold?

"What are you grinning about? You look like you're the cat who's just got the cream."

"Oh no, Sandra. I've not got the cream at all, but we never know what the future holds and sometimes that's a good thing. Come on, let's go and tart ourselves up for the second time today. I think we're heading into the cocktail hour time for a glass of wine."

Leo and George arrived promptly at seven o'clock, having gone straight there rather than going to George's cottage first. Sandra was slightly taken back with George as he wasn't a bit like she'd imagined him to be. In fact, he was completely the opposite to Leo, not a bit camp, loud or over the top. It was the start of what looked like being a fun evening and the first time that Caroline had seen George since his makeover. She was impressed with his new look as he did look years younger, but more importantly, he looked so relaxed and happy.

"Right, Leonardo of Belgravia, come into the kitchen and help me with the dinner while Sandra fills George in on your secret past."

They laughed together as Leo thought: If only they knew the half of it.

Fortunately, the days of being young, free and single with a few bob in his wallet were behind him, and Leo was so pleased that they were.

"You look very content and happy. I'm so pleased for you, Leo. I won't lie and say I haven't missed spending time with you, but I'm so very pleased for both of you. I think you're so well suited."

"Thank you, darling. I've missed you too, but the best bit is that I don't have to put on an act with George. Most of my life I've had to be one step ahead and as you know the gay world can be very bitchy. It's survival of the fittest and if you don't stay fit and have a sharp tongue, you're slaughtered. Now none of that matters anymore and for some reason it feels like a big burden has been lifted from my shoulders."

Caroline served up a lovely meal. She couldn't have wished for a better evening and she didn't feel at all like a gooseberry. They talked about Charlotte's cottage, and how impressed Sandra was with the style of both the cottages Caroline and Leo had designed.

"Yes, style, Sandra. We've always had style, haven't we, Caroline? I think the look goes well here, but I'm not sure it would work as well in a big city."

"Well, I think you're both wasted working at that hotel. I think you should be designing for a living. Surely there's a lot more homes here in

Saltmarsh Quay which need the Caroline and Leo makeover."

"It would be nice, but we'd need to go from one project to the next and as we've just lost our builder, we'd have to find another one. No, Sandra, we've had our fifteen minutes of fame, so it's back to the hotel for us."

"What's happened to Mr Tight Jeans?"

"Sorry, I'm confused. Mr who?"

"Sandra, if you saw him you'd know what I mean."

"Sandra met John in the pub last night and today when I saw him he said that he'd bought a new house and was moving away."

"A builder shouldn't be a problem. You both know a very good one and I know I'm probably quite biased, but my son Paul's a lovely chap."

"Excuse me for interrupting, but if you've got a builder now, I've got the property! Please be careful what you both say about it though as I love my little cottage here, although I'm well aware it's slightly dated. Alright, it's a wreck which needs completely gutting and before you open your mouth, no, it does not need knocking down. It just needs a little bit of love and attention."

They all laughed about George's cottage and finally he had to admit that it was rather dilapidated as there wasn't even a proper bathroom or kitchen. Caroline said that it was too big a job and if they did it they would still need another one to do after that as there'd be no way they could afford to both give up their jobs."

"Now come on, we've all had a drink. A lot of the world disasters have been caused by decisions made when drink was involved and it's not like me to be sensible, but even I know our limitations. Let's change the subject before we actual convince ourselves we are the new Kelly Hoppen!"

"Who's Kelly Hoppen?"

"Oh, George darling, I've still got so much to educate you about the important things in the world. She's only the queen of all designers."

They all laughed and the topic of conversation changed. Sandra was happy because if Leo and Caroline did decide to renovate the cottage, Paul could be involved and that would be the start of Caroline falling back in love with him. Something that was so sad and bleak in her life a few months back was now beginning to look a little better.

Leo had never really asked George much about his past, but Sandra was different. She was intrigued about George and surprisingly he revealed that his London home had been his grandmother's. She had lived to a good age and was the same generation as the late Queen Mother whose circles she mixed in. When his mother had passed away, she had taken George under her wing and just like George she also had no time for his father, her son. George had spent years living with her and she had ensured that he would be looked after financially, which had upset her son. While she was alive, George's life had consisted of accompanying his grandmother to functions and being her right-hand man. He didn't have a problem with this at all, but it had stopped him from creating a life for himself.

"I'm a great believer that everything in life happens for a reason and sometimes we can't figure any of it out. Yet eventually even if it takes months or years, it does all come together for the good."

It had been a lovely evening and everyone retired to their beds feeling very happy and content with their life. Secretly, Sandra was hoping it was a stage nearer to getting the two most important people in her life back together again.

Chapter 14

Paul couldn't wait to hear all about Sandra's weekend and she was very excited to tell him all about it. It was her mission to get him and Caroline back together and although she knew it might take some time, she felt that it would happen eventually. Sandra didn't stop talking about how much she loved Saltmarsh Quay and how safe she felt there with its lovely, peaceful atmosphere. It was just like being on holiday. Paul, however, looked sad. He didn't need to be told how he had destroyed his life with Caroline, but Sandra was determined to keep him positive and away from the gambling.

A few weeks later, George invited Caroline down to London with Leo for a few days. As he would be working some of the time, he thought they could go shopping together in London. Caroline was delighted as she loved both the shops and the theatre and couldn't wait to see George's house as Leo had told her so much about it. When they arrived, George was still at work so Leo gave her a tour of the property.

"It's magnificent! I can't get over it. There's a morning room, library, parlour! Who has a parlour these days? It's amazing!"

"Yes, I agree. It's out of this world, Caroline, but also out of this century. Just think what the two of us could do to it if we had the money."

"Leo, yes, but with a house this size you'd need millions. For a start it needs all new plumbing and electrics and that's before you begin on anything else. I think you need to forget about any ideas of doing it up. To be honest, I don't think we could do it anyway. This house needs an expert on period homes. The last thing you would want to do is to lose its character features and charm. I think we ought to stick to seaside cottages."

When George got back he insisted on taking them out to a posh restaurant for dinner. George asked Caroline for her opinion of the house and how it could be brought more up to date, and she told him exactly what she'd said to Leo.

"Seriously, George, I think a project like that would take a couple of years as well as millions of pounds. Just think of the stress involved. No thank you!"

"By the way, I'm sorry but I have to go to a dinner tomorrow night. I've manged to get a couple of tickets for a little private show if you'd be interested. Here are the invitations."

"That's a very posh envelope, George. Oh my God, Caroline, you won't believe what I've just seen. Thank you so much, George. You know it's our thing. I really can't believe it!"

"Come on, Leo; tell me, what is it? Your jaw's almost on the table!"

"Well, my darling, tomorrow 'Carolina and Leonardo Designs' are going to the private viewing of the new Lipson store in Chelsea. It's the American company's first UK store and all the top designers in the sector will be there!"

"George, thank you so much. I've read so much about this as all the interior design magazines have been discussing it for months. I know we'll never be able to afford any of the stock, but God you won't be able to stop me rolling on the rugs and cuddling the cushions. As for the furniture and china, oh, this will be the highlight of my year."

"But, darling, what do we wear?"

"A smile, Leo. A smile!"

The following morning they were out looking for fabulous outfits that would be perfect for the occasion without looking as if they'd tried too hard. Leo plumped for a dark navy suit with a crisp white shirt which would look good without a tie. Caroline settled for a red dress with a navy jacket. They both kept pinching themselves, difficult to believe that this was the designers' night of the year and they had invitations. George went off in his dinner suit to a boring banking function and Caroline and Leo called a taxi to take them both to Chelsea. They were as excited as two children going to Disneyland.

The taxi was in a queue of others gradually moving forward and eventually came to a stop outside the venue. A doorman opened the door for them and welcomed them in. Once they had showed their invitations they were handed a glass of champagne. There was so much to take in. Caroline spotted hundreds of goody bags and staff greeting everyone with a smile and offering directions to each department.

"Leo, there're five floors of deliciousness! Let's start at the top and work our way down. I don't want to miss a thing."

They soon realised that the night was purely for designers and people in the interior design business rather than celebrities. They both felt as if they were frauds being there as no one knew them although everyone was very friendly and engaged in conversation about the products. Caroline was nervous, but Leo was in his element. He was Leonardo, the premier Norfolk designer, and fair play to him, he really could hold his own among the guests, coming across as a very influential designer. A very handsome American chap came over to speak to them and Leo addressed him in his normal over the top manner.

"Hi, it's so nice of you to come tonight. We're so pleased with the turn out. Which part of the design sector do you work in?"

"Thank you. We're thrilled to have been invited. I was only saying to my business partner, Caroline, that it will be wonderful to have Lipson's in London. We won't have to keep travelling to the States anymore. Oh sorry, I forgot to mention, we're both interior designers. You might have heard of the Quayside Chic look we created."

"Of course I have. I'm told it's going to be very big in the States. Do you have a business card available?"

"Caroline, do you have any? I seem to have given all mine out."

"No, sorry, Leonardo, it seems that I have too."

The American chap was playing the same game as Leo, but he did hand them his card and asked Caroline to give him a call when she was next in New York. Caroline felt slightly angry with Leo, but it didn't matter as they would never be mixing in these circles again. As she went to put the business card in her bag, she laughed to herself.

"What's so funny?"

"You'll never guess his name. Perhaps I should visit him in America after all. Put it this way, he does fit into the pattern of how my life's going. Paul, John, then there was your George and now we have Ringo."

They both laughed so much. It had been a fabulous night although, without complaining, they wondered how George had managed to get the invitations in the first place. Back at the house they couldn't wait for George to return and to tell him all about their wonderful evening.

"God, look at you two! I think you've both had far too many additives. It would be silly of me to ask whether you've had a good time."

"Thank you so much. The products were fabulous, but the atmosphere was incredible."

"I'm off work tomorrow, so while you're coming down from such a high, think about what you'd both like to do."

The following morning Caroline was up first so she made herself a coffee and took it into the library. This was the first time in her life she had ever been to anyone's private home which included a library. It was obviously a room that had not been touched for decades as she noticed that the most recent book in there must have been at least 30 years old. It was such a beautiful room with a reading table positioned by the window and also a study area for correspondence. Caroline knew this was certainly a very special house, but not a home. It had all been about George's grandmother keeping up appearances. Oh, how times had changed. As she returned to the kitchen she could hear that the two men were now up.

"Good morning. What a wonderful room the library is. I find the way everything is categorised totally fascinating."

"So, what would you both like to do today before you have to catch your train back to Norfolk tonight? Shops and even more shops?"

"No, not for me, George. I can't speak for Leo, but I'd love to hear all about the history of your family. Just imagining your grandmother in this house and the life she must have led, intrigues me."

George was keen to talk about his ancestry. It was very rare for anyone to ask about it, let alone be interested and he walked Caroline around the house, pointing out the paintings of his predecessors and the places they'd lived in. Leo wasn't as interested and began to prepare them all some lunch. Just like the books in the library, he was sure that the kitchen utensils and equipment were more than 30 years old too. They had lunch in the morning room rather than the dining room and all laughed about the cut off time for each room. George then asked them both to come into the study with him. Neither thought there was anything strange about that until they walked in. George sat at his desk and there were two chairs opposite him. Caroline felt as if she were in the headmaster's office at school, ready to be told off.

"I've brought you in here to discuss a business proposition, so hear me out. I'd like to employ you both to renovate my cottage in Saltmarsh Quay. I know it needs more than a coat of paint and I'd like us to treat this as if it were a business transaction and I'm your client instead of us all being friends. The difference is, I don't know how I'd like the cottage transformed so you have completely free rein. However, I do have one request and that's to create a bathroom upstairs. I realise one of the bedrooms will have to go, but that's not a problem. There'll be no mate's rates for this project. This is a business transaction and you both need to earn something from it."

"George, how exciting!" We'll do a wonderful

job, I promise. When can we begin?"

"Slow down, Leo. We're a long way off starting. We haven't even taken the project on yet."

Caroline explained how the whole cottage would needed gutting, rewiring, plastering and the bathroom moved upstairs. Her biggest issue was who was going to do the work. She and Leo could design it and could provide soft furnishings and decoration, but what budget would they be working to? Caroline knew the answer Leo would have and he would be correct. Paul would be the perfect person for the building work and he would jump at the chance.

"Right, George. This needs a lot of careful thought as it's not straightforward on many levels. I think Leo and I need to discuss it and come back to you. Also, once we leave the study, I think the meeting ought to be finished and the subject dropped."

"Caroline, this is why we should be in business together. You're the brains and I'm the heart – not forgetting the glamour and the frills."

Chapter 15

On the train journey back to Norfolk, Caroline soon realised that Leo would take on George's cottage renovation whether she was involved in it or not. She needed to decide whether she'd be disappointed not to be included in on the project and eventually knew that yes, she would be. It was an enormous undertaking and while they could both do a fabulous job with the designing, they needed someone they could trust to do the work.

"Caroline, you're miles away. What are you thinking?"

"You know exactly what's going on in my head. It's George's cottage. I would love to do it, but there are so many things to consider. I don't want to discuss it until I've slept on it and thought a few things through, if that's alright with you."

Back at the hotel neither of them mentioned the project for the next few days. They both had plenty of things to think through and were secretly planning what they wanted to create for George, jotting down ideas, and sketching. After about a week, Caroline suggested that Leo came and stayed at Saltmarsh Quay for a night so that they could discuss the project.

"I've come up with a plan of action and to be honest I can't believe we didn't think of it before. It's so obvious. You and I are a team. We both do different parts of the project, so I suggest we design the cottage together and then contact Paul. We know he'll do a fantastic job, but I want you to be the one who has the meetings and discussions with him. That way, I don't need to see him. What do you say to that, Leo?"

Of course, Leo didn't have any problem with that as he just wanted to get the project underway. They spent the rest of the evening at George's cottage talking about their plans, ready to run their ideas through with him when he was next due to visit the quay at the weekend.

***

Sandra was so pleased to see Paul come home from work with a smile on his face, but she didn't want to pay too much attention to it. Secretly she hoped he was beginning to feel better about his life, but when he told her his news about Leo asking him to come and quote to transform the cottage, she couldn't have been more excited.

"This is it, Mum. I'm going to prove to Caroline how I've changed."

"But what's Caroline got to do with this cottage? It's Leo and George you'll be working for."

"Yes, but you know how Leo likes to go on and on. He happened to mention that I would not be quoting the price to George directly, but to a company called Chic Quayside Designs which is obviously something that he and Caroline are doing together. Oh, Mum, I won't mess up, I promise you. I don't know how long it'll take, but I'll win her back, I know I will."

Over the next few weeks Paul had lots of discussions on the phone with Leo as well as at the cottage, but not once did he see Caroline. Leo always just said that he needed to come back to him on things as if he had to agree it with someone else.

Finally, after weeks of negotiating, the designs were finalised, the price was agreed, and a starting date with a six-week time schedule was confirmed. George was over the moon with the plans, although to be honest, he would have been happy with anything they decided upon. Caroline was excited about the project as she knew the price would be good. She had also guessed that Paul's main objective was to win her over, but as long as the work was done, his intentions and feelings were of no concern. She had moved on.

Over the next few weeks they cleared the property of all the unwanted furniture, curtains and carpets and stored George's personal items until the cottage was just an empty shell ready for Paul and his team to start work. Caroline had purposely rostered herself on shifts when she wouldn't be at the quay at the same time as Paul would be there and when she got back in the evenings she would be able to call into the cottage by herself to see their progress.

Three weeks in and the third bedroom had been converted to a bathroom with a shower and a bath, the upstairs area had been plastered and the cottage was ready for decoration to begin downstairs. A new kitchen had been fitted, the old bathroom had been knocked down and everything was made ready for a conservatory to be added. As Paul's price for the project was so good they were going to employ a decorator. They were getting to the final phases of the project with ordering new furniture. It was so exciting!

Caroline's new routine was becoming a very familiar one. She would arrive back at the quay around six o'clock in the evening, check that both Paul's van and all the workmen had gone and then go in and see the work that had been done. She would phone Leo and talk about how much she loved the whole project. George had agreed not to come for weekends whilst the renovation work was being carried out and both Leo and Caroline wanted it to be a big surprise when he saw it for the first time.

Leo spent time in London dragging George around china shops and trying to get him excited about cups, saucers and plates, but George didn't share the same enthusiasm. He kept telling Leo to buy whatever he wanted as it was going to be his home too.

The weekend had arrived and Caroline wanted to experiment with some paint colours in the bedrooms. She knew that Paul and his team wouldn't be there and so had planned to take her time and really get the feel of the cottage. Packing herself a little picnic, she set off and by the afternoon she had tried several tester pots, taken photographs and emailed them to Leo. They had agreed on a soft grey colour for the master bedroom and a Wedgewood blue for the guest room. As the downstairs area would be one large room, they decided to keep it all white to start with and once they were living there Leo and George could decide whether they'd like to inject some colour into it.

Just as Caroline was packing her things up to go, there was a knock at the door. The last thing Caroline wanted was someone who wished to see what was going on, but there, standing on the doorstep, was John.

"I thought I could see you through the window. Are you going to be redesigning all the houses here on the quay?"

"No, this is only the second one and by the way it belongs to Leo's other half. Would you like to come in?"

Caroline could feel the butterflies in her stomach. John smelt lovely and in his tight T-shirt and jeans he looked so hot. Here she was covered in paint looking like she had been pulled through a hedge backwards. She showed him around the cottage and he was impressed with the work they'd done.

"You two really have a knack of turning something quite small and poky into a fabulous home. You should give up the day job and do this."

"Thank you, we both love doing it and we've created our own style which seems to work very well in these cottages."

With that he licked his finger and wiped some paint from Caroline's cheek. Her body shuddered with excitement. She thought back to the sex she'd had with him previously. God, it had been good, and at that precise moment that's what she wanted.

"So, John. Not out with the girlfriend today?"

"No girlfriend today or any other day at the moment. The last one wanted to settle down, have babies and play happy families. You know me, I like to have fun and that didn't sound like fun to me. I'm free, single, with no commitments and ready for some fun."

Caroline knew exactly what sort of fun he wanted and there was no way he was going to be in control of this situation. If fun was to be had, she was going to call the shots."

"Well, young man, if it's fun you want, you'd better get up the stairs and get out of those tight jeans before I rip them off."

An hour later, walking back to her own cottage, she contemplated her successful afternoon. The paint had been chosen and there were two very satisfied people. Fun without commitment was good. After showering and getting something to eat, she settled down to browse the Internet for ideas for George's garden. She needed a style that would involve little maintenance as the cottage would be empty during the week, but at the weekends it had to look amazing. Several hours later she had list of plants that didn't need much watering and had created a very modern look with a charming seated area where George and Leo could relax and enjoy the lovely mild Norfolk evenings.

The next morning Caroline got ready to tour the garden centres and nurseries. George's garden plot was small, but he was prepared to pay up to £5000 for everything, from new pathing to furniture, and Caroline thought it was achievable. Just as she was about to leave, there was a knock at the door. If it was John wanting more fun, she was ready to refuse him.

"Oh, hi, Paul. What are you doing here? I didn't realise you were working on the cottage today."

"I'm not. I just thought it's about time you gave me your opinion on my work. I know Leo says everything is fine but..."

"Oh yes, we're both delighted with everything."

"So, can I come in and chat about it?"

How could she say no? She made them both some coffee and they chatted about each room and what was left to do. Paul sat there like a little puppy being praised for doing things right, but

Caroline knew she needed to keep this professional. Surely he knew that it was he who had ended their marriage. How did he think she felt about it?

"I'm sorry. I'm not really asking you to leave, but I do need to get the garden design sorted today. The last thing I need is my builder shouting because the paving slabs haven't arrived."

"Your builder would never shout and do you know why? It's because he loves you more than ever. He's lost you, but wants you back. Please think about it, Caroline. We were so good together. I promise you we could make it work again. Things are different now."

Paul told Caroline about the casino night at the hotel and although she was so pleased for him she had seen it all before. Once Paul started to feel happy and comfortable he would have another bet which would lead to another and so on.

"I'm sorry, Paul. I need to get this garden sorted. I haven't had a day off for ten days. I'm really sorry, and I do love you, but it wouldn't work and you know that."

Caroline drove off and Paul sat in his van thinking about the words Caroline had said. "I love you" was all he needed to hear. He knew it wouldn't be easy, but he was on another rung of the ladder and would settle for that as time was on his side. With slow, gentle steps he knew he would get there eventually.

Chapter 16

At last the project was completed and George would finally get to see the makeover of his cottage. Secretly, Caroline and Leo were more excited. As long as it had an upstairs bathroom George would be happy. Caroline had stepped back a little from the final preparations as Leo was going to be living there and so it was only right that he should choose the art work, rugs and cushions. However, she was extremely proud of the garden as she had researched and designed it by herself and had loved every second of planning it all.

George was arriving at lunch time and Leo had arranged a buffet. Caroline had asked whether Sandra could come along too if Paul was invited as it wouldn't make it look like three happy couples. As it was a warm day, they could leave the conservatory doors open, making the patio look part of the cottage. The cushions outside were the same as those inside. Everything had been carefully planned and put together and the final look was so exciting.

Caroline was going to wait until Leo showed George around, but she received a call telling her that he was refusing to go in until the other half of the design company he employed was there as well. As she turned the corner they were both standing by the front door.

"Hurry up, I'm waiting to see what delights

you've both created."

George was genuinely speechless at how big the cottage and its new intimate garden now looked. Going up the stairs the landing basked in natural light which flowed through the bedrooms. The old dark atmosphere was gone, painting the beams white had been a successful plan to lift the rooms, but the most important part was the bathroom. What could he say? He was delighted. No more getting up in the night and having to go downstairs. George was in second heaven as he sat on the edge of the bath admiring the work. Suddenly there was a knock at the door and Leo let Sandra and Paul in. To Caroline's relief they only wanted to talk about the cottage. Sandra wanted to move in, she loved it so much. Paul and George were discussing the building work, leaving Leo and Caroline smiling just like two Cheshire cats.

"We've done it again, darling. We're good, aren't we? Come on, Caroline, this is what we were born to do."

The garden buffet was a success and the champagne flowed. Everyone giggled at Caroline talking about the strange plant names and George told them all about the day he had been dragged around every china shop in London. It was a lovely end to a very exciting few months.

"Friends, I'd like you to raise your glasses to two people who have not only given me such a beautiful home, but most of all a wonderful friendship. I give you Chic Quayside Designs."

It was the perfect end to a fabulous project and as Caroline sat in her cottage reflecting on the last couple of months she did realise that none of this would have taken place if it hadn't been for Paul messing up their lives. How did she now feel about it all? Was she happier with her present life? One thing she did know was that it was now back to her hotel job for a bit of a rest as juggling the two had been extremely tiring.

George had taken a couple of weeks off work and was enjoying his new home. He was so delighted with it that he was happy to show it off to anyone who wanted to have a look. It was the talk of the quay, George was becoming quite the social host as he served drinks, lunch and afternoon tea parties in the garden. Leo had to work and George would keep himself busy around Saltmarsh Quay. Caroline got the impression George was up to something as he was being a little secretive. She didn't mention it to Leo, but she knew something was up.

It was George's last weekend before he went back to London and he invited Caroline to join him and Leo for Saturday brunch. Caroline had initially declined the offer explaining that she didn't wish to be a gooseberry in their relationship, but George had insisted that she join them for brunch in the garden. The sun was shining and it was a lovely day.

"Right, you two. I'm just going to fill the dishwasher and then we can go for a nice walk. Just give me five minutes."

As the three of them headed out of the cottage, George turned left heading inland rather than towards the coast.

"Where are you going? The sea's this way, George."

"I thought we could just have a walk around the quay for a change."

"On a beautiful day like today why would we want to walk around the streets and not the coastal path?"

"Because it's what I would like to do."

Caroline and Leo looked at each other and found it all quite confusing. They walked past the pub and the shop and up and down little alleyways. It was all a little strange. Finally, George stopped at the old butcher's shop that had been empty for quite a few years, put his hand in his pocket, took out a key and proceeded to open the door.

"Why have you got a key to this shop and what are we going in here for?"

The place smelt musty and damp and Caroline knew she was right, George had been up to something."

"Come in and close the door, or should I say, Welcome to Chic Quayside Designs!"

George explained that he'd taken a three-year lease on the shop and flat upstairs. Both of them were overwhelmed but so excited. Having their own premises was one thing, but getting business would be quite another. If this venture were to fail, it could break both of them financially and emotionally.

George continued to say that to begin with Leo didn't need to be living in Norwich any more now that the cottage had been completed. Their next project could be the flat upstairs which could be rented out to bring in an income and as well as taking on extra projects they could sell bespoke items in the 'studio come HQ' of the business.

Five hours later and back at George's cottage, Caroline and Leo's excitement had not died down. Plans and drawings had been laid out and paint colours chosen. Their dream had finally come true. They knew it would be hard work, but they were such a team. It had to work, they knew it could. Chic Quayside Designs had been born.

Chapter 17

After weeks of planning, the day had arrived for the launch of Chic Quayside Designs and their little show room was ready. Caroline and Leo were both excited but very nervous as what they had created was way beyond their wildest dreams. Leo had put his flat on the market, given up his job at the hotel and was now living permanently at Saltmarsh Quay. George came up every weekend and Caroline was still at the hotel because she needed a full-time wage.

It was six o'clock in the morning and the launch party wasn't until six in the evening, but both of them were already at the showroom checking their list and cleaning it for England! On the back wall were dozens of wallpaper and fabric sample books and on the huge eight-foot table in front of the samples was a stunning display of fresh flowers and more samples of tiles and paint charts. One of the side walls featured huge photographs of the projects they had completed at Caroline's, George's, and Charlotte's cottages. All the bespoke chairs, tables, and china gave the showroom its chic look. The benefit to having it there was that they didn't need to purchase any of it as it helped the crafts people who produced it. Against the other side wall were design books and magazines, mood boards and a large selection of stunning cushions. The two front window displays were kept very simple, one with just an armchair as the main feature and more mood boards and the other window with a collage of their work.

The thing they were most proud of was that apart from the electrical work, they had done everything themselves even down to laying the carpet. The one bedroom flat upstairs needed more work than they originally thought and Paul had given them a quote, but before being able to start work on it they needed to be earning money from other projects. A further exciting thing in the pipeline was that they wanted to create some branded cushions and lampshades of their own.

Everything was ready, the champagne was on ice, nibbles prepared, and the list had been checked and ticked off. The launch party was by invitation only to building companies and interior magazines, just people in the trade of interiors were going to be there. With four hours to go there was just enough time to go home, shower and make themselves look like professional designers. They were both aware of the importance of the first impression, but were under no illusion that perhaps half of the companies they had invited wouldn't arrive. Saltmarsh Quay was quite a long way from London, which is where the big guys hung out, but with any luck they might be able to get some interest in their venture from the magazines and that would really help to kick-start their new business.

Just as they were getting ready to leave someone pulled up in a van. They could see it was Monica the Norfolk potter who they had commissioned to make some bespoke china.

"Hi, you two; I thought today would be a good time to show you these. Could you give me a hand with the boxes?"

"It's not what I think it is. You told us it would be at least six months before you could get started on anything."

"Well, I thought how can you have a grand opening party and not have some of your own china? Don't get excited. It's only a few samples, not the whole range."

Caroline and Leo were like children opening their presents on Christmas morning. Monica had produced a cup, saucer, two sizes of plate, a pasta bowl and a mug all in a lovely cream colour emblazoned with CQD and their logo. They looked so classy, it fitted their image so perfectly. Monica was delighted they were pleased and the three of them made a stunning display with the new products.

"Thanks so much, Monica. This is the icing on the cake. I think we'll work so well together. You're so kind. I really hope we can bring you lots of orders. You really deserve it. Thank you."

Back at the showroom with both Caroline and Leo looking like a million dollars, although extremely nervous, it was showtime. The first guests to arrive were two people from the Norfolk News who chatted and took some photographs, followed by a local builder with his wife and daughter who was a textile designer. They all just loved their chic quayside style. During the next hour George came up. He was as nervous for them as they were themselves. Paul and Sandra could not get over how hard they both must have worked getting the showroom ready and all the bespoke craft people were there, helping to create a lovely atmosphere. The one person who Caroline didn't want to invite and was hoping wouldn't turn up was John, who had brought an accessory with him, a young tall blonde he introduced as Chloe. Caroline smiled as he seemed to spend most of the time talking to Paul. Oh, if they'd only known! Monica had left as she felt slightly out of her comfort zone, preferring to be in a room full of clay and kilns. There were a couple of online design bloggers which was helpful as these days a lot of the business came from social media and finally there were a couple of young people making notes and whispering to each other. They did not mix and chat with anyone and both looked serious.

"Hello, I'm Caroline. Thank you for coming. Have we met before?"

"Thanks for the invitation. I'm Jane and this is Mark. We're the editors of a new design magazine which we hope to launch in the spring."

They went on to explain that their magazine was

going to be very different to any currently on sale. No before and after photos, they would concentrate on the people behind the scene. What works well and what doesn't, how they come up with their styles, meetings with the clients. It would all be very fresh and new. They exchanged business cards and were hopeful that CQD would have an article in the first magazine. Before leaving, the local builder asked if he could have a meeting with them over the following weeks, so all in all it had been a most successful launch party.

Leo was just about to give a little speech when the door of the showroom opened and in walked someone who neither of them ever dreamt they'd meet again, let alone come to their showroom.

"Please carry on. You were about to say something."

Leo's confidence was knocked back slightly, but he knew he had to say something. He looked at George who looked as proud as a father at a school prize-giving ceremony.

"Thanks so much to every one of you for coming, especially those of you who have been with us through all our projects, supporting us, encouraging and wishing us well and that means so much to both of us. Neither of us know where the journey of this venture is going to take us, but we're both so excited to be starting this in the beautiful Saltmarsh Quay."

Leo glanced towards the door as the late arrival

was looking around. Caroline looked a little flustered wondering whether they should both approach him. Was he there to see their work or did he have something else on his mind?

"Good evening, Caroline. Thanks so much for the invitation. Norfolk's in such a stunning part of the UK. I'm sorry I'm a little late, but I kept asking my driver to stop so I could take a look at the views. I must say what a fabulous showroom you have. I think you both should be so proud. I'm really pleased for you."

Thank you very much, Ringo, and thanks so much for taking the time to come all this way. This must seem a million miles away from what you are used to with Lipson's."

Ringo went on to explain how he was in the UK for a few weeks working on different project launches for Lipson's. As soon as Jane and Mark realised who he was they pounced on him and to be honest Ringo was very eager to chat to them, so they exchanged phone numbers.

"So, Caroline, you have the full set all in one room, although you have only three to choose from. George is mine, but that does leave you with the other three Beatles. Which one are you going to choose?"

The last thing Caroline needed in her life at that moment was a relationship. The very casual thing she had with John was good, a glass of wine or two, hot sweaty sex and then goodbye. No sleep over or having to chat over breakfast. As for Ringo, she wasn't going to kid herself. He wasn't there to see the launch of CQD, but was there to chat her up. Caroline was extremely flattered, but how can you have a relationship with someone who spends most of their time in another country? And what about Paul? Paul was besotted with her and would do anything to get her back. However, the night was all about her and Leo's new venture. There was no time to fit any of the Beatles into the equation.

The champagne flowed and the evening came to an end and a list of meetings arranged. The guests had drifted off and the packed showroom was now empty apart from the two of them doing the final clearing up. The hard work would begin the next day as they would need to put all their time and energy into making it a success.

"Do you know the best part of this whole thing, Leo?"

"What's that?"

"It's working with my best friend, spending time with him laughing and doing what we both love so much."

"One last glass of champagne, Caroline. Here's to us. Not just CQD, but to the best friendship in the world."

Chapter 18

The evening had been a great success. Everyone had loved the showroom and the products on display. That of course was one thing, but earning money from it would be another, and now the real work needed to start. They had three completed projects under their belt, and now they had to find a fourth. Both of them were at the studio for nine o'clock. After the previous night's champagne, coffee and more coffee were the order of the day and it was down to business.

"Right. Down to business, Caroline. I've got my list from the launch. Have you got yours? I've scribbled so many notes that it won't be in the right order, but let's start from the top."

First of all the pottery from Monica, which seemed to have attracted a lot of interest. The deal with her was a lucrative one, and also similarly with Philip the carpenter as his coffee table had also received a lot of interest. The highlight of the evening was Jane and Mark's new magazine which would be a real introduction for them both onto the designer stage. They needed to set up a meeting with Frank the builder as from what they could gather he built on plots of land which were big enough for six to twelve properties. They were always sited near to the coast and most of them were second homes. They could only guess what Philip was interested in, but hopefully it would be the show home. That would be quite an easy home to refurbish as there wouldn't be any construction work needed. Fingers crossed, the possibilities for ongoing work were plentiful. Leo went to make another coffee and Caroline was sorting out the wallpaper books, which also had a lot of interest, when someone came into the showroom.

"Good morning, Caroline."

"Oh, hello, Ringo. I really didn't think we'd see you back in Norfolk again. Oh, I am sorry. I didn't mean that to sound like you're not welcome."

"No offence taken, but I haven't left yet. I stayed up at the Saltmarsh Cliff Hotel last night, so really it's still my first visit. Yesterday was a social event, but today I'd like to talk business if you've got the time to spare."

With that, Leo came out with the coffee.

"Oh, good morning, Ringo. Thank you so much for coming last night. We hope it was worth the drive and time."

Ringo went on to explain that it was more than worth it. He was very interested in their signature china and wanted to discuss the possibility of putting a few of their items into Lipson's. Obviously it would be down to the price as it would mean that three people needed to make money out of it and Monica would have to be able to cope with the volume of items needed if the project proved successful. Secondly, as Ringo was going to be staying in Saltmarsh Quay for a couple of days, he wondered whether Caroline would have dinner with him.

"I'm not going to give you the excuse that it's purely to discuss business, because I never mix business with pleasure. This is me wanting to spend time with you."

What could she say? In her mind this was all about business. Having someone like Ringo as a contact could really help Chic Quayside Designs to grow, and he was a very handsome man so why wouldn't she want to have dinner with him?

"Of course! I'd love that. Thank you. Shall we say around seven?"

With that the door opened and a florist delivered a huge bouquet. Caroline read the accompanying message: "To Caroline. Thank you for letting me be part of your new adventure, love Paul." She felt herself blushing and just as she was going to make an excuse the door opened and in walked Frank the builder.

"Well, I can see you're awash with admirers. I best get off. I'm working from the hotel today. See you at seven."

"That would be lovely. Thanks for popping in. We're both so excited, aren't we, Leo?"

Off Ringo went and Caroline didn't have the time to think or worry about the evening ahead as Frank was on a mission to get something sorted out.

"I won't beat around the bush. Obviously you've

both looked into what I do and for the last six years I've been paying a company from London to come and put my show home together. My wife and daughter have been nagging at me, telling me that they don't stand out from all the other properties going on the market, so once the places have been agreed with the council I'd like you to do everything from light switches to the kitchen. That is if we can agree on a price to suit both of us."

"I'm sure we could come to an agreement that would help both businesses. Before we start on any projects I think we should look at what you've been doing in the past and what needs changing, but yes, we'd be very interested to be involved."

"There's just one other thing. As you know, my daughter has just finished her textile degree and I've offered to set her up in some sort of business. However, I'm not one to waste money on things which I don't understand, and I need some advice on the best way forward on this. I feel that you both are ideally placed to help me."

They agreed to give some thought to it and planned a meeting with Frank and his daughter for the following week. He was waiting for planning permission on a plot of land 15 miles away, which was likely to take some time. Leo and Caroline were very excited about the possibility of this new venture, but they knew that if they were to secure the contract they had to come up with something for his daughter. The day was flying by with phone calls from bloggers and magazines wanting interviews. As the day finally drew to a close, there was just one more job left to do and that was to phone Paul and thank him for the flowers and then for Caroline to get ready for her date.

Caroline was quite excited about having dinner with Ringo. She did find him very handsome, although it wasn't his looks she was after, but his expertise. He had been at the top of his game in interior design and retail for years and she certainly wasn't going to let this opportunity go to waste. Alright, she might flutter the eyelids, but there was no way anything else was going to happen.

Caroline loved going up to the hotel as the staff were friendly and the food was to die for. As for the view, it was the icing on the cake.

"Hello, Caroline, how was your day? Busy I hope after last night's launch. I must say Saltmarsh Quay is so special and I love this hotel. The only problem is that I haven't been able to get any work done today as I find myself just staring out to sea. It's so mesmerising."

"I know what you mean, and I never take it for granted. I feel very blessed to be living in such a lovely place."

They went into the bar and had a pre-dinner drink where Caroline told him all about her day. Ringo agreed with her that staging a show home was a very good business move as the amount of footfall over a period of time would be far more valuable to the business than adverts in magazines. He explained how it would become the bread and butter that would lead to their bespoke work.

Over dinner they talked less about careers and more about themselves. Caroline didn't explain the full details of her break up with Paul but used every opportunity she could to try and pick Ringo's brains on design. He was very open about himself. He lived in New York, but was only ever in his apartment for five days a month as he travelled all over the States and also spent time in Paris and London. There wasn't a wife or a partner involved, not even a cat.

"The thing is, Caroline. I love my job far more than I love being in a relationship. I'm not saying I don't like female company, but I think you know what I mean. I realise I'm probably barking up the wrong tree here with you so let's enjoy the evening and I'll let you carry on interrogating me with everything interiors."

"I'm so sorry, Ringo. It's just that your knowledge and experience is something I'll never have the opportunity to learn about again."

'I think we both know what we wanted out of this evening, so let's just enjoy ourselves with no strings attached."

Ringo was very honest with Caroline and explained that if she and Leo really wanted to hit the big time with their business they would have to move to London. However, the unique style they had created was the new, fresh chic quayside look and the industry was always on the lookout for new ideas.

"No, we don't want the stress of the big time and to be honest we're both too old for that. If we can make a living from the business, we'll be more than happy."

"Well, I think you're both on the way to doing that. It must be so good to have a relationship like you two have. You're the best of friends and you work together, and as long as you stay true to your look I really think Norfolk will have some fabulous properties that you'll be able to feel very proud of. In a way I feel very envious of both of you."

"Why's that? Look at your life, the success you've had and the exciting life you lead. You should be so proud of yourself too."

"Yes, I agree with all you say, but there's one word missing in my life and that's 'contentment'. I've never sat back and felt happy with my lot. I'm always chasing something and I really don't know how it feels just to be satisfied with life."

"Perhaps you need to make some changes to your life. Do you really want to be travelling the world? Is New York the place you want to live or is it time to take stock and rethink what you want out of life? The thing to remember is that this isn't a rehearsal. You get one attempt and then it's over. I'm so sorry, if that sounds harsh. It's really none of my business."

"No, perhaps you're right. There is more to life than work. I just need to find out what it is or who it is."

After that they both turned the conversation around to lighter matters – family, friends, holidays, childhood memories, all things away from the present time. The evening had been a lovely one and as Caroline got into the taxi and waved goodbye she considered that although this was a man with the world at his feet, would she want to swap places with him? Her answer was quite simple. No, what she had here in Saltmarsh Quay was so very special to her.

Chapter 19

'Hi, Mum, I'm home. How was your day?"

'Hello, Paul, not too bad. I haven't done much. Still recovering from last night's champagne. You're late. How was your day?"

Paul explained that Caroline had phoned to thank him for the flowers and that she and Leo had been busy with enquiries. He had managed to have a chat with Keith, his right-hand man, who had worked for him for 15 years.

"I don't want to talk about it right now, Mum, in case I put a jinx on it, but I think I've come up with something and I'm nervous, but excited."

Sandra told Paul how she would be spending both the following day and evening with Caroline after she finished her shift at the hotel. They would be going out for something to eat and then enjoy an evening at the cinema.

Over at Saltmarsh Quay Leo had finally stopped telling George about his day. To be honest, George didn't mind, he was just so happy to have Leo in his life that he could talk about anything he wanted to.

"George, we're both so grateful you gave us the opportunity to live our dream and I promise we won't let you down."

"I know you won't. Both of you are so talented. I just hope you won't be so busy that it stops us spending time together. There're so many places in the world I'd like to visit I haven't bothered to go to in the past, but now I have you in my life, I want us to have fun, lots of fun."

Back at the hotel the following morning, Caroline felt quite envious of Leo being in the studio while she was sitting in front of a computer working out room rates and special offers. She hoped the shift would pass by quickly as she was looking forward to catching up with Sandra, having a girly chat and a meal out.

Ringo had cancelled his visit to Paris and was staying on at the hotel for another couple of nights. He hadn't slept well, spending most of the night staring out the window watching the moon shining on the sea. Caroline's words about life not being a rehearsal had a big effect on him and so Ringo intended to take stock of his situation. What better place could he find than Saltmarsh Quay?

Leo's morning was going very well. He'd had a couple from London call into the showroom who had just bought a house in Saltmarsh Quay. The problem was they could only see the sea from the bedrooms and the downstairs felt very cramped. They wanted to know what they could do to lighten the place up. Leo was in his element but explained that he couldn't really advise them until he'd seen the property for himself.

"Come on. I'll switch the answer machine on and put a note on the door saying I'll be back in an hour. Let's go and have a look."

Leo had only been in the cottage five minutes when he came up with a solution. It wouldn't be a cheap option and he would have to work out his costings, but this first meeting was all about creating the dream for the couple.

"This is such a lovely property with so much potential. If it was mine I'd turn it upside down and make a living room, dining room and two bedrooms, put the bathroom in the kitchen and convert the upstairs into one big space. Take the two bedroom windows out and put in doors with Juliet balconies and you can look out to sea for miles."

The couple were amazed. It was an obvious thing to do, although they did need to think about it back in London. They left the key with Leo so that he could work out a quote for doing the job. The plumbing, normally the expensive part of renovations, didn't need to be adapted as would just be a question of switching around the kitchen and bathroom. Leo was confident he could convince the couple and then this would become their first official project.

Back at the showroom Leo was soon on the phone to Paul to see if he was free to quote for the job. He knew he would because it meant he could see Caroline.

"Yes, that's fine. I'll meet you at the cottage at around five. Have you got any idea what the clients want to do to the place, or is it just a lick of paint?

"No, it's not just a lick of paint and no, they don't know what they want, but I do. I just need to persuade them that's what they want."

***

Sandra caught the bus to meet Caroline. She really loved the time they spent together and was so pleased that it had continued despite Paul and her splitting up. First on the agenda was a meal before going to the cinema. Caroline couldn't wait to tell Sandra all the latest news from Saltmarsh Quay and how excited they were about the possibility of doing the show homes for Frank, although she was still puzzled as to what to suggest for his daughter.

"Did you say she's just finished a textile degree? Why not ask her to come up with something to add to your signature range of china, cushions, and napkins. I'm sure there's something."

"Oh, Sandra. You're a genius. Yes, tablecloths and tea towels. That's just perfect."

The rest of the meal was spent thinking of everything from hats to put onto boiled eggs, to throws, blankets and bedding. They got so involved in their discussions that they were late for the start of the film.

At the quay Paul and Leo spent a couple of hours going over the cottage and estimated that the job would be quite straightforward. Changing the windows to doors would be cheap, but everything else would be down to the quality of finishes that the couple wanted.

"Hello, how was the cinema, Mum?"

"Good, thanks. We've had a lovely time. What have you been up to?"

Paul told Sandra about the new project at the quay and how he hoped to get the job. Sandra was delighted as it looked like he was putting the past behind him and life was beginning to improve.

Chapter 20

Caroline was up early for the next few days. She didn't need to be at the hotel until five in the evening and Leo was taking a day off from the business, so she was spending the first day by herself. Leo had phoned to tell her the news about the couple from London and Caroline was thrilled to bits to hear of their first real project. She logged into her emails and couldn't believe how many there were. Messages from local carpenters and blacksmiths asking if they could display their work and more bloggers wanting interviews. It was all so exciting. The showroom door opened and there stood Ringo.

"Hi, I was hoping you were here. I just popped in to say goodbye and most of all, to thank you."

"You've nothing to thank me for it. It should be the other way round, me thanking you for all the help and advice as well as perhaps the opportunity to have our china displayed in Lipson's."

"No, Caroline, I need to thank you. I'm off back to the States. I'm taking a month's holiday in California and at the end of it I will decide what I'm going to do with the rest of my life. Somehow, I don't think it will involve much travelling. I think I'd like to have a home to go back to every day instead of just a couple of days a month."

Ringo was in full flow when in walked John who was visiting his parents and wanted to see how

Caroline was getting on. He really knew how to raise her temperature even on a cold day as there he stood in a tight white T-shirt and even tighter jeans. As Caroline was introducing them, the door opened again and in came George who just called by to bring Caroline a cream cake on his way back.

This is turning out to be quite a party, she thought. All she needed now was for Paul to walk in and she'd have the full set. As if on cue, in Paul came and her embarrassment suddenly turned into a fit of laughter. The four of them just stood there staring at her without saying anything. The more they stared at her, the more she couldn't stop laughing.

"None of you get it, do you? I'm so sorry, I'm not laughing at you all, but I just find it so amusing that I'm stood here with The Beatles – there's John, Paul, George and Ringo."

One by one they left to go on their separate ways. First to go was George and then John who seemed to get the message there would be no fun today. Paul explained that he had only dropped in to leave a quote for the job and finally Ringo said his goodbyes and hoped they could keep in touch.

"I want to be able to call you at some point, hopefully soon, and tell you that I'm finally content with my life. Thanks, Caroline, for pointing me in the right direction and please, if ever you want to pick my brains, just drop me an email."

With that he was off, and Caroline was relieved.

What a morning she'd had. Now it was back to business: answer some of the blogger's questions, look at some of Frank's other show houses online and go over Paul's quote.

***

The next few weeks flew by. The couple from London agreed on most of the plans for their cottage, but weren't sure whether they wanted to keep the kitchen separate from the living space. They would make that decision once the two bedrooms were knocked into one. Leo and Caroline had viewed the floor plan for Frank's new show home and were coming up with plans and ideas for that as well as commissioning his daughter, Sarah, to come up with samples for tablecloths and tea towels. They had also taken on two small projects decorating holiday flats in the next village, so things were really beginning to look good. However, the most important news was that Caroline had cut her hours at the hotel by half. She was delighted with this. The hotel didn't want to lose her completely but allowed her work her 120 hours per month however she wanted to – either as over a fortnight or spread over the month. George and Leo had gone on holiday to France.

Although Caroline had to admit she was tired, life was working out well, not just for her but for Leo too. The future of their business looked very promising and given time she might be able to give up her job at the hotel. As she poured herself a glass of wine and started to cook some pasta she thought of Ringo. He was a really nice fellow and she hoped that he could sort his life out. Stirring the sauce into the hot pasta, she wondered what delights George and Leo would be eating in France but knew that Leo would be paying more attention to the restaurant decor than the menu and would no doubt return with plenty of ideas. As she went to close the curtains she could see John driving towards his parents' house. Even the urge to have him pop in had disappeared, all her needs and wants had been replaced by Chic Quayside Designs. Oh, how things can change in your life in such a short time.

Just as she finished her pasta there was a knock at the door. Oh no, she thought, he's going to be so disappointed. Best he goes off to one of his other lady friends. But as she opened the door she was surprised to see it wasn't John, but Paul instead.

"Hi, Caroline. Is this a convenient time? There's something I'd like to talk to you about."

Paul went in and Caroline poured them both a glass of wine. She could tell he was nervous and ready to get something off his chest, but strangely for the first time since they had split up, she felt relaxed and comfortable in his company although she wasn't exactly sure why.

"I want you to be the first to know this and I've

not even told Mum yet. I'm getting rid of the building company. Keith's taking it off my hands. I don't need the worry and the stress anymore. I've had enough of it. No more invoices and bills. Any of the work outstanding that I've already quoted for, Keith will give me a fair percentage of and he's also paying me for bits of equipment."

"But what are you going to do? You still need to earn a living."

"I'm a good tradesman, Caroline. I can turn my hand to most things and there's this hot new interior design team here in Norfolk who seem to keep needing a reliable builder and decorator, so I'm putting all my eggs in one basket and hoping they'll keep employing me."

"It's a long time since I've been called hot, but yes, Paul, you know we'll give you work if we have it. Are you sure that's what you really want though?"

"What I really want is my wife back. I miss her so much and I'll do anything to get her back."

"But, Paul, can we turn the time back? Can we go back to how things were?"

"Caroline, I don't want to go back to how we were. That's the time I was lying to you. The gambling has stopped now and to prove to you that I've taken control of money, you pay my wage and give me pocket money for petrol and sandwiches. I want things to be different, a fresh start, new beginnings."

"You know I've never stopped loving you, Paul, but I can't go through all of that rubbish again. I really can't."

"Caroline, please give me a chance. Why can't we start by doing things together like going out for the odd meal and going to the pictures or just going out for a walk together? That's something we both love doing, so please could we start by being friends?"

"We've never stopped being friends so perhaps that's the place to start, but I'm telling you now that if you ever hurt me again it's not just the friendship that will end. You'll never get any more work from Chic Quayside Designs.

Chapter 21

EIGHT MONTHS LATER

Leo and Caroline were on the train returning from London. They were so excited as they'd had a fabulous day. Whoever would have thought they'd be launching their bespoke china in Lipson's? They were thrilled about it, not just for themselves but also for Monica. The sample of tablecloths from Sarah appeared to have attracted a lot of interest and hopefully would soon be on sale as well.

"Can you believe it, Leo? Look at us! I know it's a one-off, but we're sitting here in our first class compartment drinking champagne."

"No, my darling. We've worked so hard to get here that I'm not travelling any other way ever again. I still pinch myself at what we've achieved and there's not a day goes by when I don't read that headline:

"FORGET LONDON, NEW YORK AND PARIS – THE HOT NEW DESIGNS ARE COMING FROM NORFOLK!

That's what they're saying about us, the two ex-hotel receptionists who are the talk of the interior design world."

"Yes, it is quite surreal to think we're now in the position of picking and choosing the work we want to take on, not to mention how our order book is full for at least another year and a half."

"I know, and to think how many of those top building companies we've turned down. Really I think it's not just down to hard work. We've stuck to our guns and kept to our trademark look. That's what people love, our chic quayside style."

"But, Leo, it's not just our professional lives that have been successful. There's you and George so much in love and having a fabulous time together. Could you ever believe you'd be so happy?"

"No, that was never on the cards for me. My life was all about being out on the town and having fun. How different it all is now. Whoever would have thought you and Paul getting back together would ever happen either? Everything's for a reason. If you'd never split up, Chic Quayside Designs would never have started out."

"I know, and things are better than ever with Paul. Our only problem was his gambling and I truly believe he has put that behind him forever. The other thing is having Sandra living in the flat above the showroom, there's nothing more she loves than giving us days off and holding the fort. We really do have the perfect life."

"No, my darling. None of this would have happened if we didn't have the perfect friendship."

THE END

Also by Ian Wilfred

Putting Right The Past
The Little Terrace of Friendships
A Secret Visitor to Saltmarsh Quay
Secrets We Left in Greece

Printed in Great Britain
by Amazon